diary of a
REAL PAYNE

TRUE STORY
[WITHDRAWN

Annie Tipton

BARBOUR
PUBLISHING

© 2013 by Barbour Publishing, Inc.

Print ISBN 978-1-62416-131-5

eBook Editions:
Adobe Digital Edition (.epub) 978-1-62416-453-8
Kindle and MobiPocket Edition (.prc) 978-1-62416-452-1

Cover illustration and design: Luke Flowers Creative

Published by Barbour Publishing, Inc., P.O. Box 719, Uhrichsville, Ohio 44683, www.barbourbooks.com

Our mission is to publish and distribute inspirational products offering exceptional value and biblical encouragement to the masses.

ecpa Member of the
Evangelical Christian
Publishers Association

Printed in the United States of America.
Dickinson Press, Inc., Grand Rapids, MI 49512; August 2013; D10004052

To my parents:

For always believing in me.
And for giving me the confidence to
use the gifts God has blessed me with.

Dear Diary,

Hey, hi. How's it going? (I never know how to start things like this.)

Let's be honest: It's weird that I'm writing a letter to a blank book inside of that blank book. I know you can't write back to me, Diary, but here I am, writing to you. Why? Because Mom thinks keeping a diary will be a "good outlet" for me. What does "good outlet" mean? I have no idea. I know there's a "bad outlet" in our guest bedroom. I found it last week when I plugged the vacuum in and it wouldn't turn on. Mom thought I was just trying to get out of chores (again), but the outlet really was broken. It did get me out of vacuuming for a few minutes, though. I counted it as a big win for EJ. Who's EJ? That's me. Emma Jean Payne. EJ for short.

Since I'm going to be writing in you a lot, Diary, let me tell you a little bit about me: I'm 10. I've got freckles on my nose, elbows, and knees. My eyes are light green and my hair is. . .well, my hair is hard to describe. The best way I know how to explain it is that it's shoulder length, not-quite-blond-but-not-quite-brown and not-quite-straight-but-not-quite-curly. ALL of that is bad enough, but here's the worst part: Mom keeps my bangs trimmed a little too short because she hates it when hair falls in my eyes. The second she sees me blowing my bangs off my face, her scissors appear out of nowhere for a "trim" that ends in a bangs massacre.

My hair is basically a tragedy.

I'LL be in the fourth grade at Spooner Elementary School this faLL. Spooner, as in, Spooner, Wisconsin—the single most boringest place in the universe. I wish I was kidding, but I'm not. For a town that has an entire museum that's "dedicated exclusively to the heritage of the canoe," the word boring might even be too nice.

Here are the things I love:

1. My family. Dad's the pastor at Vine Street Community Church. He loves God, and he loves people. And he loves games. If he were a superhero, his superpower would be that he could make a game out of anything. This one time, when we were standing in a hugely long and boring line at the grocery store,

he made a game out of guessing how many candy bars were in each box at the checkout. He even got some of the other people waiting in line to play. An old man wearing flannel, who had a scraggly beard tucked into his belt, won the game in a tiebreaker by correctly guessing there were eleven Butterfingers in the box. Dad let him pick out any candy bar he wanted as a prize. You would've thought the guy had won a new car, he was that happy. I don't think I'll ever forget the wide grin on that whiskery face as he clutched the king-size Snickers in his fist.

Mom teaches second grade at Spooner Elementary. There are a lot of great things about her, but one amazing thing is her hair. It's long and blond and beautiful and perfectly straight, and she puts it up by twisting it into a knot and sticking pens in it (or pencils, or chopsticks, or big paper clips, or whatever else is handy—we never know what she's going to find in there!). Once on a Sunday morning right before the worship service was about to start, Mom saved the day by fixing the busted button on Dad's pants with a red pipe cleaner she found in her hair. Why was there a pipe cleaner in her hair? Pipe cleaners were part of the kids' church craft that morning—and it did a great job keeping her hair out of the way. Thanks to Mom's sweet hairdo, Dad preached that morning without worrying that his pants would end up around his ankles.

I have a Cockapoo mix named Matthew Cuthbert T-Rex Payne, but I call him Bert for short. Mom and Dad gave him to me as a puppy for my eighth birthday, and even though Bert is my dog, they made me let my little brother help name him. So I gave the first two names (Matthew Cuthbert is a character in Anne of Green Gables—more on that superb work of fiction later), and my dork of a brother loves dinosaurs, hence "T-Rex." (Seriously, though, what kind of a name is that for a dog? A dumb one.) Some dogs look like they're smiling and other dogs may have a bored-looking face, but Bert is different. He has at least ten unique feelings he shows on his face. Here are my favorite six:

1. Happy—"It's playtime!"
2. Guilty—"I'm sorry, EJ. . . . Mom's begonias looked like they wanted to be dug up."
3. Hungry—"If you don't feed me that piece of bacon from your plate, I literally will fall over and die of hunger this very moment."
4. Curious—"What is it? What does it smell like? What does it taste like? Can I play with it? Can I? Can I? Can I?"
5. Proud—"I saw that you left a bag of trash sitting on the kitchen floor, so I figured that meant you wanted me to help you sort through it. As you can see, I did a great job shredding the bag and organizing what was inside, all over the floor. You're welcome."
6. Loving—"EJ, you're the bestest friend a pooch could ever ask for. Can we snuggle and watch movies?"

Bert is an adventurer at heart, and he's game for anything. As dogs go, he's fantastic.

And then there's Isaac. I do love my little brother, but there are some moments I'm not sure I like him. He's five and about to start kindergarten. He likes dinosaurs and cars and dirt and boy things and being nauseatingly cute with his blond curls and little-boy smiles. He knows one joke, and he tells it ALL THE TIME.

Isaac: Knock-Knock.

Willing Participant: Who's there?

Isaac: Noah.

Willing Participant: Noah who?

Isaac: Noah good joke? (Outburst of crazy laughter that goes on entirely too long for such a lame joke.)

I call Isaac "The Space Invader" because that's what he does—gets up in my space—every moment of every day he possibly can. Mom says he likes me and just wants to play with me. I say he just wants to annoy me until I snap.

2. Reading. I read cereal boxes, comic strips, books, magazines, encyclopedias—I love it all! My favorite books are Little House on the Prairie (How cool would it be to travel in a covered wagon like Laura Ingalls Wilder?), the Chronicles of Narnia (Every time I see a wardrobe, I have to open the door and stick my head inside. Hey, Narnia could be just behind those hanging clothes!), Little Women (Confession: I've only seen the movie of this one, but it's on my list to read!), and Anne of Green Gables (Anne Shirley's carrot-colored hair might be even more tragic than mine).

3. Dreaming. Not sleep dreams (although some of those are pretty great, too) but pretending, imagining, traveling to another time and another place with just the creativity in my mind. Mom and Dad encourage me to be imaginative, but they've been on this kick lately of telling me to "be where you are when you're there, EJ." I'm still not completely sure what that's supposed to mean, but I do admit that I spend a lot of time daydreaming about. . . well. . .everything! I imagine the big, important, amazing

adventures that are just waiting for me when I'm an adult and can get out of here. See, here's the deal: My plans are bigger than Spooner, Wisconsin. There are so many things I want to be and do that the list is already five notebook pages long (front and back— college ruled!). And the truth is, what I want to be when I grow up changes at least twice a day. It's a big, beautiful world, Diary, and I want to experience all of it!

So here's to this new thing I'm trying—writing in you, Diary. Hold on to your hat. Or your spine. Or your cover. Or whatever it is a diary has to hold on to. It's going to be an adventure!

EJ

Chapter 1

CAUTION FLAG

Dear Diary,

Sunday afternoons are reserved for naps in the Payne house—and rightfully so. After a busy morning at church where Mom teaches a classroom full of preschoolers about Jesus' love in kids' church and Dad preaches about Jesus' love to adults in the worship service, they end up snoozing on the couch after lunch. I have way better things to do with my time than sleep, so I usually endure the parent-enforced quiet time by reading a good book.

Last Sunday, Dad was watching the NASCAR race on TV when he dozed off. Truthfully, Diary, when I heard Dad's breathing turn a little snore-y, I planned to ever-so-gently remove the remote from his hand (I'm really good at the game Operation. Even the nearly-impossible-to-remove funny bone is no match for my expert surgeon skills) and turn the channel to something better. But just before I was able to hit the number for Disney Channel, the race cut away to a profile of female race-car drivers, and I got sucked into their fascinating world.

Did you know that the first women NASCAR drivers raced in 1949? How cool is that? Three ladies named Sara, Ethel, and Louise drove in some of the very first NASCAR races ever. And since then, lots of girls have raced around stock-car tracks, hitting speeds of nearly two hundred miles per hour in superfast cars. One girl named Johanna entered a truck race when she was just nineteen, Diary! Nineteen! Just think. . .nine short years from now that could be me—the cheering crowd zooming past my window as I round the bend toward the checkered flag for my first-place finish!

But for now Mom's putting the brakes on my racing career by making me go back-to-school shopping for jeans and No. 2 pencils. What an absolute snooze-fest. I hear her calling for me to come get in the minivan so we can leave, Diary, so I'll say good-bye for now.

But seriously. Racing—why didn't I think of this before?

EJ

EJ looked down at the paper in her hand and sighed.

LIST OF NECESSARY SUPPLIES FOR ALL STUDENTS
ENTERING MS. PICKERINGTON'S 4TH GRADE CLASS
AT SPOONER ELEMENTARY SCHOOL:

1. 3 packs of wide-ruled notebook paper
2. 50 No. 2 pencils with 40 pencil-top erasers
3. 4 solid-color spiral notebooks (NO DESIGNS on notebooks)
4. 1 black-and-white composition notebook
5. 6 solid-color pocket folders (NO DESIGNS on folders)
6. 2 bottles of glue or 4 glue sticks
7. 1 (24-count) box of crayons
8. 2 large boxes of facial tissues
9. 2 bottles of hand sanitizer (8 ounces or larger)
10. 1 container disinfectant/cleaning wipes (10 ounces or larger)

"I think this is the most *UNinspiring* school supply list anyone could've imagined, ever in the history of lists," EJ moaned from her seat behind Mom in the family minivan.

"Let's tone down the dramatics a bit, EJ," Mom replied with a hint of a smile in the rearview mirror. "Fourth grade is an important year of big firsts, and based on the supply list, it looks like you'll be writing quite a bit. You'll like that, won't you?"

"I guess," EJ said, shrugging. She wanted to say, *I don't know how creative I can be with four drab notebooks that don't have designs on them. Or how I'll be able to truly create art with a measly twenty-four crayon colors to choose from,"* but she decided against it and looked out the window at the passing houses instead.

The first day of school was just two and a half weeks away. As much as EJ enjoyed school, she was still a little nervous about being in Ms. Pickerington's class.

"Mom, the kids call her *Ms. Picky* for a reason," EJ said, fastening the bottom button of her green-and-purple plaid shirt, which she'd somehow missed. (Mornings never were EJ's best time of day.)

"Being picky isn't necessarily a bad thing," Mom replied. "Do your best, and I'm sure you will get along just fine with Ms. Pickerington."

"Marmalade, I'm getting finger paint for kindergarten?" Isaac asked from his booster seat next to EJ, tapping the head of a plastic toy brontosaurus on the window. Ever since Isaac could talk, he'd called Mom "Marmalade"—secretly, EJ knew it was pretty adorable, but she'd never let her brother know that.

"You betcha, buster," Mom said as she pulled into a parking spot at Family Saver Superstore. "Hopefully we'll be able to find everything we need for back-to-school this morning. And then. . ."

"Lunch at the park!" EJ finished Mom's sentence with a grin.

"Yeah! We're going to eat brontosaurus meat for lunch!" Isaac shouted gleefully and started gnawing on the dino's tail.

"*You* are disgusting. Who knows where that thing has been!" EJ said, wrinkling her nose.

"He's just being a boy," Mom replied.

"Yum!" Isaac added.

⭐

Forty-five minutes later the school supply aisle was crowded with frazzled moms, crumpled supply lists in their hands, trying to herd their hungry kids. But EJ's mom didn't let little things like back-to-school shopping stress her out. After all, if she could handle a classroom of twenty-five second graders hyped up on heart-shaped sugar cookies and red punch at a Valentine's Day party, shopping for new pairs of jeans and bottles of hand sanitizer seemed pretty easy.

Mom pulled a purple pen out of her hair and crossed through "thick, washable markers (8 count)" and "finger paint—yellow, blue, and red" on Isaac's kindergarten list.

EJ leaned against the shopping cart handle and eyeballed a notebook with a cover that had multicolored stars all over it. *One black-and-white composition notebook*, her brain reminded her. EJ rolled her eyes.

"I think we've found everything except for glue that's on both of your lists," Mom said, double-checking the papers in her hand.

"Tabby—hi!" a woman gushed as she waved at Mom from the end of the aisle. The woman steered her cart toward the Paynes, and EJ saw it was Liz McCallister, a lady who went to their church. EJ grasped the shopping cart handle and tried to blend in with the school supplies on the shelf behind her.

"Liz, so nice to see you!" Mom said, tucking the purple pen back in her hair for safekeeping. "Where are CoraLee and Katy?" CoraLee was in EJ's class at school, and Katy was about to start kindergarten, just like Isaac.

"Oh, honey, they're home with a sitter." Mrs. McCallister made big motions with her perfectly manicured hands as she spoke. "I can't imagine bringing the children shopping at a place like *this*. We try to avoid Family Saver when we can. It's just so crowded and dirty, and it attracts the wrong kind of people."

Mom opened her mouth to reply that it's the best place in Spooner to stay on budget, but Mrs. McCallister caught EJ's eye and forged on.

"Oh, EJ, I see you're still in your tomboy phase—jeans and

plaid and those canvas sneakers you *always* wear." Mrs. McCallister
shifted her attention back on Mom. "CoraLee absolutely will
not leave the house without wearing a skirt or at the very least
something pink with ruffles. And of course Katy wants to be just
like her beautiful big sis. Just think, when I have two teenage
girls—I'll have my hands full!"

"Sounds like it—" Mom got cut off as Mrs. McCallister
snapped her neck back toward EJ.

"CoraLee is just *so* excited about being in Ms. Pickerington's
class this year. She's serious about her studies, and we've even started
discussing colleges for her. Have you started yet, EJ? You really
shouldn't wait much long—ow! What? . . . Hey, stop that!"

"Rooooooawwwwwrrr!" Isaac growled as his brontosaurus toy
poked Mrs. McCallister hard in the shin from Isaac's perch on the
rack under the shopping cart (his favorite place to hide during trips
to Family Saver).

EJ crouched down, grinned at Isaac, and whispered, "Nice job,
Isaac."

"Isaac! Stop that right now." Mom used her serious voice. Not
the you're-in-trouble-and-will-be-punished-when-we-get-home
voice, but the one she uses when it's time to stop messing around.
"Tell Mrs. McCallister you're sorry."

The dino peeked its head over the top of the cart and said in a
high, squeaky voice, "I'm sorry."

"Well, that's okay," Mrs. McCallister said to the brontosaurus,
patting it awkwardly on the head. "Looks like maybe it's time for
the dinosaur's lunch. See you Sunday, Tabby." Mrs. McCallister
gave Isaac one more uneasy look before shoving her cart in the
other direction.

"Now. . .glue," Mom said, her attention back to the task at
hand. "I don't see it in this aisle. Maybe they have it in a special

spot for back-to-school. Isaac, come with Mom and let's see if we can find it. EJ, follow us, okay?"

Isaac grabbed Mom's hand and shoved the dinosaur in his jeans pocket, leaving the head sticking out so it could see what was going on.

As the three rounded the corner, EJ caught a glimpse of the black-and-white checkered design of a chessboard in the toy aisle.

Chessboards look a lot like checkered flags, EJ thought. . . .

"Gentlemen, start your engines!" the voice echoes over the loudspeaker at the racetrack.

"Hey! I'm a girl*!" EJ shouts out the window of her car.*

"Oh, right. Sorry, EJ," the voice responds. "Girls, start your engines, too."

EJ flicks the ignition switch, revving the engine to life, and flips her helmet shield down into locked position. As the youngest race-car driver in the history of the sport, she knows the eyes of the world are on her. She tugs on her leather gloves and makes sure her protective jumpsuit is zipped all the way up.

She glances out the window of her car and sees a wall of spectators cheering for the start of the race. Some even waving signs to cheer her on:

America's Favorite Racer—EJ Payne!

EJ's a Real Payne If You Try to Beat Her!

EJ—Faster Than Lightning!

Real Girls Drive Fast!

There's a flash of green as the starting flag is waved, and EJ slams the accelerator to the floor—her car is off like a shot. Around the first turn she eases off the gas a bit and then gains spectacular speed in the straightaway. With such an amazing start to the race, EJ is sure to bring home a first-place finish.

Suddenly over the sound of the roaring engines, the crowd erupts into a rhythmic chant for its favorite racer: "E-J! E-J! E-J! E-J! . . ."

But what's that? A yellow caution flag so early in the race? EJ thinks she must be imagining things. She raises her helmet's shield to get a better look, and sure enough she sees the caution flag—but not any normal caution flag. It's a woman standing in the middle of the racetrack, waving a yellow scarf like a maniac. "What is this?" EJ mutters. She stomps on the brake, bringing the powerful car to a screeching halt inches away from. . .

. . .a six-foot-tall display of glue bottles.

"EMMA JEAN PAYNE! What do you think you're doing?" Mom's voice definitely crossed the line into you're-in-trouble-and-will-be-punished-when-we-get-home territory. The cart rolled a few more inches and bumped into the display, scattering a dozen glue bottles on the floor.

"I was. . .uh. . . racing," EJ muttered down at her toes, still trying to shake off the vivid daydream she'd been yanked out of. "Youngest race-car driver ever."

Just then Mrs. McCallister walked past and glanced at the scene with an annoyed look. EJ thought she saw Mom's face flush a bit, but Mom quickly stuffed her yellow scarf in her purse and kneeled down to pick up the glue bottles from the floor.

"I called your name over and over when I saw you 'racing,'" Mom said. "But you didn't respond. Thank goodness I was wearing my yellow scarf today, or we really would've had a sticky end to the race."

"Sticky!" Isaac said, laughing. "Good one, Marmalade!"

EJ helped pick up glue bottles and stack them on the display, relieved that Mom didn't seem *too* upset. "I'm sorry, Mom," she said quietly. "I didn't mean for that to happen."

"I know, EJ. We'll talk about it later," Mom said. "By the way, how was the race going when I threw the caution flag?"

"I was in the lead," EJ said, giving Mom a small grin to test the waters.

"I don't doubt it." Mom smiled. "Now how many of these glues do we need again?"

⭐

Isaac had already gobbled up his chicken nuggets (or "brontosaurus nuggets" as he called them) and half of his carrot sticks and was hanging upside down on the jungle gym when Mom took her first bite of grilled chicken salad. Finishing her cheeseburger, EJ wadded up the sandwich wrapper and tossed it into a garbage can a good eight feet away from her seat at the picnic table.

"Three points," Mom said. "With skills like that, you might follow in my footsteps as the 1990 middle school female basketball player of the year."

"You were player of the year—really?" EJ asked.

"You don't have to sound so surprised," Mom said with a twinkle in her eye. "I had an early growth spurt and was the tallest in my class in sixth grade. Then everybody else caught up with me after eighth grade, and my short-lived time as a basketball star was over."

"I bet that was disappointing," EJ said, munching on an apple slice.

"Not really," Mom said.

Isaac bounded up to the picnic table, excited, out of breath, and a little sweaty in the August heat. "Mom, that kid over there *(inhale, exhale)* says there's a big anthill and that the ants will carry food back to their families *(inhale, exhale)*. Can I feed them a carrot?"

Mom reached over to his four abandoned carrot sticks and picked up two. "You may feed one to the ants if you eat this other one right now," she said, handing him the carrots.

"Deal!" Isaac chewed up one carrot stick, turned to EJ, and said, "This carrot tastes like fish. Get it? See-food?" Then he stuck out his tongue to show EJ the mushed-up orange pulp. Mom and Isaac laughed.

"Not funny, goofball," EJ said, trying to hide a smile.

Isaac ran off toward the anthill, and Mom called after him, "Make sure you break up the carrot into little pieces so the ants can carry them home!"

"Are all little brothers as gross as that one?" EJ asked.

"Oh, absolutely," Mom said. "But you need to give him a break, EJ—he just wants your approval. It's okay to laugh with him sometimes."

"I'll keep that in mind," EJ said.

Mom sipped her cherry cola and raised an eyebrow at EJ. "Hey, we need to talk about what happened at Family Saver earlier."

"Oh, I know what you mean!" EJ perked up. "It's a good thing Isaac's brontosaurus got hungry when he did. It really got Mrs. McCallister to leave in a hurry—"

"No, not that. I'm talking about your shopping-cart race," Mom said.

"Oh," EJ said, shrinking a little on the picnic table bench.

"EJ, you know that your dad and I love your creativity. We want you to dream big, and we want you to learn and read about places and things so that you can use your imagination," Mom said.

EJ sighed, knowing there was a "but" coming.

"But sometimes you have to be aware of what's actually going on around you," Mom said, pulling the wadded-up yellow scarf out of her purse and tying it around her neck in a loose bow. "If this scarf hadn't snapped you back to reality, the finish line might've ended up all the way across the store in the dog-food aisle."

EJ smiled to herself, imagining a photo finish that resulted with a busted bag of dog food and Bert up to his eyes in kibbles, his tail wagging happily.

"EJ Payne takes the top honors in today's race, sponsored by K-9 Kibbles," the announcer says. *"And nobody's more excited than her sidekick, Bert!"*

"EJ. . .earth to EJ!" Mom snapped her fingers in front of EJ's glazed-over eyes. "Don't ignore all of the great things that happen in real life, too."

"There's nothing great in Spooner, Mom," EJ said, kicking a clump of grass with the toe of her Converse All Stars. "Exciting things don't happen here."

Mom smiled and scooted closer to EJ on the picnic bench. "Do you believe that God has plans for you, EJ?"

"Yeah, I do, Mom—" EJ started.

"I do, too, sweetie," Mom said. "And I also believe that God has plans for EJ Payne that are better than even her *amazing* imagination can dream up."

"Hey! Guys!" Isaac shouted from across the playground, waving his arms to get their attention. "You gotta come see this! Two ants are dragging an entire hamburger patty back to their family!"

"Sounds pretty spectacular." Mom glanced sideways at EJ. "Wanna go check it out?"

"An entire hamburger patty?" EJ looked skeptical. "That'd be like Isaac picking up the swing set over there and carrying it home. This I have to see."

Chapter 2

MRS. WINKLE

August 9

Dear Diary,

Mom and Dad are celebrating their twelfth wedding anniversary by spending a night and a day in Minneapolis—so guess what that means, Diary? Isaac and I get to stay overnight with my very favoritest neighbor ever, Mrs. Winkle!

Mrs. Wilma Winkle lives next door. She's grandma-age, but her husband died before I was born and she doesn't have any kids or grandkids of her own. She doesn't let that get her down. She told me once that in God's family she has precious children (like my mom and dad) and grandchildren (like me and Isaac). And even though we're not related to her by blood, that doesn't make any difference. "God knows just what we need," she says, "and that's why He brought your family next door to me when you were a baby!"

Before Mrs. Winkle retired, she was the art teacher at Spooner Elementary. She is one of the most creative people I know.

She has a very unique sense of style (but really, who's to say that a yellow-and-purple sweater paired with orange pants isn't fashionable?), and she decorates her house with all her own artwork and fascinating craft creations.

One of my favorites is a ceramic fruit bowl in her kitchen that she painted with pictures of colorful fruit—grapes, strawberries, blueberries, kiwi slices, bananas, apples. Inside the bowl on the very bottom she painted a picture of her own face, grinning up at anyone who takes a piece of fruit from the bowl. According to Mrs. Winkle, she's just saying "good job" on choosing a healthy snack.

The other great thing about Mrs. Winkle is that her imagination is almost as vivid as mine. I'm looking forward to seeing where our creativity will take us this time. Now if only Isaac doesn't ruin it. . . .

Time to go pack my suitcase!

EJ

Mrs. Winkle shut the front door and spun around to face EJ, Isaac, and Bert. Bert, a big fan of Mrs. Winkle, hopped happily around her knees until she stooped to pat his furry head.

"So, my dearies, your parents are on the road to Minneapolis, and we have the whole night ahead of us," she said. "What's on the schedule tonight?"

"Hmmm." EJ plopped down her red polka-dot overnight bag on the floor in the living room. "We could play Scrabble."

"Scrabble—check!" Mrs. Winkle said as she rolled up the sleeves of her flowy red dress with tiny black top hats and canes all over it. "What else? Come on, let's get *creative*. . . ."

EJ looked around the room for some inspiration. Creativity was something Mrs. Winkle was really good at—from the jungle-themed couch she painted herself to the dozens of tiny stuffed animals hanging from the ceiling fan by varying lengths of string. ("It's an *animalier*—an animal chandelier," she'd explained with a laugh.)

"Food art, food art, food art!" Isaac chanted while he drove a toy monster truck in the middle of the living-room floor.

"As you wish, young Master Payne," Mrs. Winkle said. "To the kitchen!"

Although most adults don't approve of kids playing with their food, Mrs. Winkle had always encouraged it. "Food has so many lovely colors and textures," she'd said when she introduced EJ to food art. "Meals shouldn't have to look the same every time."

Food art had only one rule: whatever you use in your masterpiece, you must eat.

Past food-art sessions included

✧ extra-lumpy mashed potatoes that were great for sculpting busts of American presidents (although Isaac's Abraham Lincoln ended up looking more like a

T-Rex with a beard and a top hat);
✧ french toast sticks cut into bricks to construct
Buckingham Palace and a moat filled with syrup
("Buckingham Palace doesn't have a moat, but if the
queen could have one filled with delicious syrup, I bet
the old girl would dig one herself," Mrs. Winkle said);
✧ hamburgers and french fries meant abstract paintings
out of ketchup, mustard, and relish (that one was so
delightfully messy);
✧ pancake batter squeezed from a bottle onto a hot
griddle became a game of "What animal does this
pancake look like?" followed up with new paint
brushes to dip in chocolate syrup and honey to add
the details to the cow or fish or bird;
✧ make-your-own-pizza masterpiece with an array of
toppings (Isaac discovered a newfound love of green
peppers when he used them to make Yoda).

Tonight, though, something entirely different: chicken sticks
that made perfect logs for building an early American settlement of
cabins surrounded by a forest of broccoli trees.

"I think it's the best we've ever made," Mrs. Winkle said,
adding one more broccoli tree to a row of shrubbery on the
northwest side of town. "What shall we name our settlement
before we eat it?"

"What about. . .Monster Truck City?" Isaac whipped his toy
from underneath the table and started to cruise through the small
pathways between the cabins, making little-boy truck noises.

Mrs. Winkle snatched the truck off the table before it could
touch the food. "Good thought, Isaac, but there were very few
monster trucks in eighteenth-century America, and none that were

properly de-germed to be around food," she said.

"Pinkletonville!" EJ blurted, the idea just coming to her. "It's our last name and your last name, plus a little more to make it sound like the name of a town."

"Pin-kle-ton-ville," Isaac said, pronouncing each syllable slowly. "Where dinosaurs play with the children!" T-Rex promptly popped onto the table and peeked into a log-cabin window, whispering (in Isaac's voice), "Who wants to play hide-and-seek, kids?"

"What a positively perfect name for such a creation," Mrs. Winkle said. "But I'm hungry after all this building, so let's pray and dig in."

After stuffing themselves on Pinkletonville and the surrounding forest (Mrs. Winkle even let Bert in on the action by making a little building out of bacon-flavored treats on top of his bowl of kibbles. "Every settlement needs a fort in case of dinosaur attacks," she said), they played a game of Scrabble.

But not *any* game of Scrabble—the *Winkle* way of playing. For normal Scrabble, you can only play words you can find in the dictionary. In Winkle Scrabble, you can use real words *or* completely made-up words. Made-up words just have to follow two rules:

1. The person playing the made-up word must be able to pronounce it.
2. The person playing the made-up word must be able to give it a definition.

After a game that was neck and neck between Mrs. Winkle and EJ, Isaac came out of nowhere to use his last tiles to make the word *zowquad*, using a triple-word tile and a double-letter tile on the *q*, earning him seventy-eight points. A zowquad, according to Isaac, was a four-headed cow from Neptune. EJ never thought the Winkle Scrabble rules were dumb until that very moment.

While Mrs. Winkle was putting the Scrabble board away, a book on the coffee table caught EJ's eye: *Aristocrazy Through the Ages*.

"Mrs. Winkle, there's a spelling mistake on this cover." EJ held up the book and pointed to the first word in the title. "Isn't this about kings and queens—*aristocracy*?"

"Ahh, I see you've found my favorite book," Mrs. Winkle said as she sat on her jungle couch and patted the cushion next to her. "It's all about *crazy* things kings and queens have done throughout history."

EJ sat on the couch and opened the book across her lap to take a better look.

"Crazy? I was crazy once," Isaac said, looking up from the living-room floor where he was playing with Bert. "They locked me in a big, white room. I died there. Then the worms came. . ."

"Oh boy, here we go. . ." EJ sighed.

"Worms? I hate worms! Worms drive me crazy. Crazy? I was crazy once—" Thankfully Isaac took a breath between sentences.

"Excellent story, Isaac," Mrs. Winkle interrupted his never-ending tale. "But there are a few folks in this book that make even crazy you seem absolutely normal. Come see."

Isaac and Bert sat on the other side of Mrs. Winkle and settled in.

"Here's one about a Russian tsar named Fyodor the First," Mrs. Winkle said, pointing at a picture of a man pulling down on a rope. "The people called him Fyodor the Bellringer because he wandered aimlessly through Russia, obsessed with ringing every church bell he could find."

They read about a Bavarian princess named Alexandra who

thought she swallowed a glass piano, and a Mexican empress named Charlotte who had living chickens tied to the table legs in her hotel room.

"There are crazy stories in the Bible, too." Mrs. Winkle flipped a few pages. "Ever heard of King Nebuchadnezzar?"

"Isn't he the king that threw Daniel in the lions' den?" EJ asked.

"Yes, and he also threw Shadrach, Meshach, and Abednego in the fiery furnace, but those aren't the nuttiest stories about old Nebby," Mrs. Winkle said. "He was a very proud king with a huge ego. In fact, his ego was so big and out of control that after many warnings from God that his pride would lead to bad things, Nebuchadnezzar eventually went insane for a time."

EJ read aloud from the book:

Nebuchadnezzar:
The Wild-Animal King
Daniel 4

King Nebuchadnezzar stood on the roof of his royal palace in Babylon and surveyed his empire. Pleased with himself and his accomplishments, he boasted, "Look at this great city of Babylon! By my own mighty power, I have built this beautiful city as my royal residence to display my majestic splendor."

After he had said these words, a voice called down from heaven, "Nebuchadnezzar, as of this moment, you are no longer ruler of this kingdom. You will be driven from human society. You will live in the fields with the wild animals, and you will eat grass like a bull. You'll live this way until you learn that God is the One who is in control and has mighty power—not you."

Within that same hour, Nebuchadnezzar was cast out to live in the wild—grazing on grass like a bull. He lived this way until he had long, scraggly hair and his fingernails grew out so they looked like bird claws.

"Eww, weird!" EJ grinned.

Isaac hopped off the couch onto all fours, pawing at the ground and snorting like a bull. Bert joined him, barking playfully.

"My brother has gone completely insane," EJ said. "It was only a matter of time."

"I'm fresh out of hay for you, Mr. Bull," Mrs. Winkle said apologetically.

Isaac responded with a disappointed "moo" and rammed an overstuffed footstool with his head.

"Here's another story I think you'll like." Mrs. Winkle turned to the next page, an entry titled "Xerxes: The King Who Bowed to Peer Pressure."

Mrs. Winkle started to read:

In ancient Persia ruled a king named Xerxes. He was an okay king, but he was far from perfect. One night at a big party, the king bragged to his friends about how beautiful his wife, Vashti, was. "The rarest jewel in all the land," he assured them. "I'll bring her out to dance for us and you'll see for yourself what a stunning creature she is."

"What does he think I am? A prized pig for him to parade in front of his horrible friends?" Queen Vashti snapped at the servant sent by King Xerxes. "Tell him I won't come to fulfill his stupid request."

"And that's when he banished her," EJ said, remembering the story from kids' church. "That's dumb! Vashti was just sticking up for herself."

"Very true, but that's the way Xerxes chose to rule Persia," Mrs. Winkle said. "Apparently he was influenced pretty easily by others—sometimes for evil and sometimes for good."

"Oh yeah! Haman!" Isaac piped up from the floor where he was pretending to chew his cud. "He was the bad guy, right?"

"Bad to the core," Mrs. Winkle said. "His peer pressure on the king almost meant the murder of all the Jews in Persia." Mrs. Winkle turned a few more pages to an entry titled "Queen Esther: One Gutsy Chick."

"But, thankfully for the Jews, they had Queen Esther to influence the king for good," Mrs. Winkle said.

EJ stared down at the page, soaking in the picture of the beautiful young woman. She traced the outline of Esther's long, flowing dress that looked like it was made of fourteen layers of light material that would flutter when she moved through the palace courtyard. Esther, with her olive-colored complexion and lovely dark hair, looked so different from EJ, with her freckles, sort-of-blond hair, and green eyes. But there was something behind the eyes of Queen Esther. . . What was it? Fear? Maybe. But she also looked confident. Like she had made up her mind and was ready to go for it. . .whatever *it* might be.

Queen Esther-Jean (EJ for short) looks down at her hands and starts to nibble on a hangnail. Before the king picked her out of the many women to be the new queen, she had been through twelve whole months of beauty treatments, where they took care of things like hangnails. Now that those treatments are done, she takes care of manicures like she always did before: with her teeth.

A servant steps into Queen EJ's chamber and says, "Your highness, Mordecai is here to see you."

"Yes, of course, please show cousin Mordecai in right away." EJ smooths her dress and straightens her royal headpiece. Work on the hangnail will have to wait. "Thank you."

A kind, old face enters the room. Mordecai is Queen EJ's cousin, but he is more like a father to her because he raised her after her parents died when she was a baby. Slightly stooped, with a face full of wrinkles, his eyes are as bright and alive as a young man's. In a very unqueenlike moment, EJ jumps up and sprints across the room to hug her dear Mordecai.

But it's not a moment of joy for the queen. She is sobbing on Mordecai's shoulder.

"There, there, dear one." Mordecai holds EJ close. After a few moments, EJ begins to speak.

"Mordecai, I thought I was ready. I thought I was brave enough to ask the king to spare our lives—the lives of the Jews," she says, wiping away tears with the back of her hand—exactly NOT the way she was taught to do it in beauty school. "I had a meal prepared, and the king came. I was all ready to ask him, but then that evil man—Haman—showed up, too. I felt like I had been punched in the stomach and all the air was out of my lungs. I couldn't make the words come out of my mouth."

"But your servant tells me you have another chance tonight at a second meal with the king." Mordecai's eyes sparkle. "EJ, you have already been so brave. This is just the big finale you've been waiting for."

"I don't know if I can do it," EJ says.

"By yourself? You can't," Mordecai responds.

"Thanks for the encouragement, cousin." EJ flops down on her throne, not caring that she's crumpling the back of her dress.

"Hear the words I'm saying." Mordecai takes a step toward EJ.
"You can't. But it isn't all about You. The truth is that the God of our fathers, Abraham, Isaac, and Jacob—the God who spoke the heavens and the earth into being—the God who has chosen you to be His special, beloved child, EJ—put you in this very time, this very circumstance, to do something great for Him. He will work through you. Let Him be brave through you. You're just along for the ride."

"God is doing great things through me," EJ whispers to herself.

"That's right, my queen," Mordecai says. "Your people are praying for you. You are not alone."

☆

The delicious food is prepared, the table is beautifully set for a royal dinner for three—the king, the queen, and the king's adviser, Haman. EJ stands at the table, waiting for her guests to arrive. She tugs at a jeweled necklace that's a little too tight and nervously fiddles with the gold bangles on her wrist. She may never get used to these clothes.

Suddenly, the door opens and the two men come in with a flourish.

"My darling EJ, so happy to have dinner with you two nights in a row!" the king gushes at EJ.

"Queen." Haman nods toward EJ, sneering slightly.

"Welcome," EJ says, gesturing to seats for both men. "On tonight's menu, one of my favorites: pigs in a blanket. Made, of course, with the finest turkey hot dogs in all of Persia."

"Turkey?" the king looks confused. "Don't the royal cooks usually make pigs in a blanket with pork hot dogs?"

"Yes, your majesty." EJ takes a deep breath and continues. "But that leads to the real reason that I have asked you to come here tonight."

"Anything you want, EJ," the king says. "Just ask."

"You see, I asked the royal chefs to prepare tonight's meal in the kosher tradition, keeping with laws that God has asked my people to follow," EJ says, gaining more confidence with each word.

"Your people. . ." Haman looks horrified, knowing what's about to come.

"I am Jewish. And this man"—EJ points at Haman—"has plotted to kill me and thousands of my brothers and sisters. If his plan succeeds, my people will be completely erased from the earth. . . . Please do not let such a thing happen, King Xerxes!"

"Bravo!"

Mrs. Winkle's standing ovation snapped EJ back into reality. Finding herself kneeling on the floor, her hands together in a pleading gesture, she blushed and crawled back to her seat on the couch. Apparently Mrs. Winkle found her behavior completely normal.

"The king's heart was softened toward Queen Esther's request," Mrs. Winkle said, putting an arm around EJ. "The Jews were saved and Haman—"

"Haman got killed instead!" Bull-Isaac rammed the footstool again for dramatic effect.

"What do you think of Queen EJ, er, Esther?" Mrs. Winkle asked with a wink.

EJ thought for a moment before answering.

"She was kind of like a Bible superhero—saving all those lives," EJ said.

"I've always thought of her as a 'yes woman,' " Mrs. Winkle said. "There was an opportunity in front of her to do something good and she said yes. No matter what, that's a good place to start."

Mrs. Winkle checked her watch. "Heavens! It's past ten. It's time for all bulls, queens, and 'yes women' to be in bed!"

EJ stood and picked up her overnight bag. "Mrs. Winkle, may I sleep on the waterbed tonight?" she asked. "The last time I slept there it felt like I was on the high seas, and I had the very best pirate dreams ever in the history of waterbed dreams."

"As any good 'yes woman' would say. . . ," Mrs. Winkle said with a grin, "Yes. Yes you may."

Chapter 3

MY LIFE AS A SPACE CADET

August 20

Dear Diary,

Tomorrow is my first day of fourth grade. My clothes are laid out (new jeans, a new plaid shirt with blue, green, and a tiny bit of pink, and of course, my signature wardrobe item: red Converse All Star high tops). My book bag is packed with all my new supplies (don't you love the smell of a new box of crayons, even if it is only a twenty-four pack?). And my favorite lunch is packed (peanut butter and banana sandwich, string cheese, Golden Delicious apple, and a cran-raspberry juice box).

I've gotten over my nerves (mostly) and have a good feeling that fourth grade is going to be the year of EJ. I'm ready to do my best and really pay attention. Except that whole thing about paying attention is hard for me. Well, it's hard when I'm not interested in what the teacher's saying, which happens sometimes. There are a lot more interesting things going on in my head most of the time.

My teacher this year is Ms. Pinkerington.

She has a little bit of a reputation of being a stickler, Diary. I usually get along with my teachers, so I'll do my best this year, too. If I need to turn on the "ol' Payne charm" like Dad says, I will.

3+5=8

The Space Invader will be tagging along to Spooner Elementary tomorrow, too—starting kindergarten. Just when I thought I was going to get a break after spending all summer with the little booger, he's gotta go and butt in at school, too.

(Side note: I'm about 93 percent sure he's going to end up being the kindergarten paste-eater.)

Dad just called for lights out, Diary. Time for prayers and sleep. Good night!

EJ

"Have a great day, guys!" Mom called from the window of the minivan parked in the drop-off lane at Spooner Elementary. "See you at three thirty!"

EJ waved, and Isaac waved his plastic triceratops at Mom as she rolled up the window and drove toward the parking lot. Even though she taught second grade at Spooner Elementary, she always gave EJ her space at school. Mom was there when EJ needed her (like that time she got a weird rash that showed up on her forehead and Mom had to take her home—later they realized the rash was from Bert's flea shampoo. EJ had accidentally used it in the bath the night before), but on a normal day, EJ wouldn't even notice that her mom was at the school.

The sidewalk was full of nervous moms saying good-bye and crying over uncomfortable little kids. It was six short hours of school, not like the kids were moving to India. EJ never really understood the outpouring of emotion on the first day of school. Oh well, at least Mom didn't get weepy like these moms.

"Let's get one thing straight, kid." EJ looked down at her brother. "Mom said I'm supposed to hold your hand until we get to your classroom. And because today's your first day of school and Mom promised me an after-school snack of crackers and spray cheese, that's the *only* reason I'm holding your hand."

EJ grabbed at Isaac's hand, but he snatched it away before she could get a good hold on it.

"Tricycle doesn't want to hold hands," Isaac said, holding up his triceratops. "He says you have cooties."

"Tell him he can get a cootie shot from the school nurse," EJ said, annoyed. And without another word, she snatched the tail of Tricycle and yanked Isaac, who held onto the dino by the head, toward the front door of the school.

"Cooooooooooties!" Isaac howled.

"Shut it! You're embarrassing me," EJ hissed.

Too late.

"Well, if it isn't little Miss EJ Payne—already a real *pain* in the neck by causing such a scene." EJ heard a sugary voice behind her over Isaac's hollering.

"Ohhh, *real* original." EJ turned and narrowed her eyes, seeing CoraLee McCallister standing with her arms crossed. CoraLee's little sister, Katy, stood next to her, dressed in a similar pink and equally frilly dress and sparkly shoes, looking like she'd rather be wearing a paper bag than so many ruffles.

"I heard my mom say that you're a real space cadet," CoraLee continued, cocking her head to the side. "That when she saw you at the store, you had this real dreamy look on your face and you almost ran over three babies with the shopping cart. Like your brain wasn't even there."

"There weren't any babies!" EJ looked defiant, still holding on to the dinosaur tail. Isaac quieted down to watch what was happening between his sister and the fluffy mound of cotton candy named CoraLee. "I just knocked over a couple of glue bottles. I don't know what that has to do with being an astronaut. I was imagining that I was a race-car driver."

EJ regretted saying that last sentence even as it was coming out of her mouth.

"*Imagining*? You're ten years old, and you were *playing pretend*?" CoraLee laughed a little too hard. "Mom's right—you're a *space cadet* with your head in the clouds. Good luck in Ms. Pickerington's class, EJ P-A-I-N."

Grabbing Katy by the elbow, CoraLee marched her little sister toward the front door.

"HEY!" Isaac shouted after CoraLee. "It's spelled P-A-Y-N-E!"

"Come on." EJ took Isaac's hand, this time without a fight

from either of them. "Let's get you to kindergarten so you can learn how to tie your shoes and color in the lines."

★

The first morning in Ms. Pickerington's class was pretty terrible, even worse than EJ had expected:

Roll call
Ms. P: Megan Oliver?
Megan: Here!
Ms. P: Emma Jean Payne?
EJ: Here. Ms. Picky—er—Pickerington, would you please call me EJ instead of Emma Jean?
Ms. P: I will call you Emma Jean, Emma, or Jean. Not EJ because it is not your name. Also, anyone who calls me Ms. Picky will be given a ten-minute detention at the beginning of recess. This is your only warning, class.
EJ: So. . .no EJ?
Ms. P: No.
EJ: *(sigh)* Emma Jean then.

Math
CoraLee: *(raising her hand)* Ms. Pickerington?
Ms. P: Yes, CoraLee?
CoraLee: Emma Jean Payne is drawing doodles on the front of her math notebook.
Ms. P: Emma Jean, our class supply list clearly said that notebooks must be without design. This includes our own designs. Do you understand?
EJ: *(glaring at CoraLee)* Yes, Ms. Pick–Pickerington.

Spelling

Ms. P: *(looking up from her grading book)* Emma Jean, I see here that your spelling test scores were top of the third-grade class.

EJ: Yes, ma'am.

Ms. P: Well, I expect great things from you this year. Don't get lazy. Study, study, study!

☆

Finally, lunchtime! EJ carried her red lunchbox decorated with sparkly yellow stars to the packers' table and sat down to enjoy her favorite part first: string cheese.

She'd just finished the last delicious strip of white dairy goodness when her best friend, Macy Russell, plopped her brown paper lunch bag on the table and sat down.

"How's it going, EJ?" Macy reached into her lunch bag, pulled out a napkin, and placed it oh-so-perfectly on her lap. "Isn't fourth grade fantastic?"

Macy was in the other fourth-grade class at Spooner Elementary—Mrs. Cleary's class. Mrs. Cleary had the reputation of being the exact opposite of Ms. Picky. Rumor had it that her students would actually be given time in class to decorate their notebook covers ("Creativity leads to better learning!" she may or may not have said), and unlike Ms. P who kept a strict to-the-minute schedule in her classroom, EJ heard that Mrs. Cleary had a spinner on her chalkboard that students would take turns spinning to see what the class would do next. Kids said that in 2010, her class was once lucky enough for the spinner to land on "recess" five times in one day.

Macy's beautiful coffee-colored hair cut into a neat bob and sparkling chestnut eyes were only the beginning of the differences between them. Macy was one of those rare kids who just seemed to ogether. She never had a hair out of place, a shoe untied, or a shirttail untucked. EJ always felt like she needed to sit up a little straighter and wash her hands a few seconds longer when she was around Macy. But not in a bad way.

The truth was, each girl really liked the differences she saw in the other. Macy loved joining EJ on her imaginative adventures now and then. And EJ appreciated Macy's attention to detail, her logical brain, and the fact that she had a good head on her shoulders.

"Fourth grade is *not* fantastic." EJ crumpled her napkin and threw it into her lunch box. "I might be looking at the longest year of my life."

"Tradesies?" Macy smiled and held up her small bottle of strawberry milk, pointing it at EJ's juice box.

"Yeah, totally!" EJ smiled, and the girls swapped drinks. "Thanks!"

Macy carefully unwrapped the bendy straw and punctured the foil circle at the top of the box, making sure her thumb covered the end of the straw. EJ wrenched open the sealed cap of milk, spilling a drop on the table in front of her, and took a gulp that resulted in a nice pink mustache.

Macy sipped her juice and grinned. "Uh, EJ, you've got a little. . ." She casually pointed at her own upper lip and licked it.

"Oh, this?" EJ pointed with both hands at her milk mustache like it was the best thing she'd ever done. "I've been growing this for weeks." EJ and Macy laughed.

Ms. Pickerington, lunch monitor for the day, walked by at just that moment, giving EJ a disapproving look.

"Excellent. Another strike against me." EJ shrugged, using her wadded-up napkin to wipe off her milk mustache before taking a big bite of her sandwich.

"What should we do at recess?" asked Macy, changing the

subject to get EJ's mind off of her teacher. "I heard there's a new jungle gym with a sweet set of monkey bars this year." Macy had been taking gymnastics since she was three, and EJ had always been jealous of her ability to perform spectacular feats on the playground equipment. "I could show you a couple new things."

"Sounds great," EJ said. "Now if you could just give me some of your gracefulness and balance, too." EJ regularly tripped over her own feet.

Twenty minutes later, EJ and Macy gripped the monkey-bar rungs and swung their legs back and forth, pendulum style. Seemingly effortlessly, Macy swung her legs up in front of her face, hooked her feet in the bars, and let her hands drop toward the ground.

EJ grunted as she unsuccessfully tried to do the same.

"How on earth do you do that?" EJ huffed, flailing her legs in frustration.

"When you swing, you let the weight of your legs help move you forward and up," Macy explained, showing EJ again. "Seven years of lessons at the YMCA don't hurt either. Here, let me help."

Macy hopped down to the ground and shouted out instructions to her friend: "Back, forth, back, forth—up!" on the word *up*, Macy pushed on EJ's knees from behind and gave her the extra boost she needed to get her feet up to the monkey bars. "There! I knew you could do it."

EJ wrapped her knees around the bars and secured her feet under the rungs before letting go with her hands to hang upside down. She always loved how slightly wrong the world felt from this perspective.

"Have you ever thought about what it'd be like if up was down and down was up?" EJ glanced over at Macy, who had already gotten back to her upside-down spot next to her. "Would we say, 'I'm going up to the basement'? Or would basements be on the top floor and we'd still say 'I'm going down to the basement'?"

"Hmmm, I'm not sure," Macy replied. "You mean like if there was no gravity?"

First Lieutenant EJ taps the communications button on her space suit to initiate two-way communication with her flight captain, Macy. "Captain, I'm waiting for your signal to start our space walk."

"The atmosphere is clear of all space junk," Captain Macy speaks into the headset microphone while she checks the computer display in front of her. "All levels are displaying normal, and your vital signs are in the clear, Lieutenant. Other than the fact your heart rate is elevated a bit."

"I'm just excited." EJ smiles, trying to calm her racing pulse. "We've been training for five years for this, Mace."

"That we have," Macy replies. "Make it one for the history books, EJ."

Macy keys in a few last-second details, takes a deep breath, and says, "All clear and ready for space walk. In 10. . .9. . .8. . ."

EJ hears the bay doors of the shuttle whoosh open above her, and she unbuckles her safety belt. "3. . .2. . .1. . ." and just like that, the zero-gravity of space pulls her outside the space shuttle, floating into the heavens—the big blue-and-green earth above her against a backdrop of an inky black sky filled with twinkling stars.

"Oh. . .my. . .goodness." The sight takes EJ's breath away, but Macy's voice slices into the moment of awe.

"EJ, abort! Abort!" Macy yells into her headset microphone. "There's an uncharted being that just appeared on my radar screen. It looks like it is angry, EJ—get out now!"

"Mace, I just got out here," EJ says, looking around to see what Macy could possibly be seeing on radar. "I just want a few more

minutes. *Maybe it's just a broken satellite like last time.*"

"*No, EJ. . .it's not that. . .it's Pick—*" *Suddenly their radio connection dissolves into a crackle of static and dies.*

"*Mace?*" *EJ tries not to panic, pushing hard on the communications button.* "*Macy? CAPTAIN RUSSELL?*"

Silence.

EJ's breath catches in her throat. She must steady her fear or she'll start hyperventilating. She looks around, desperately trying to come up with a plan. Without communication to the shuttle, she can't get back inside.

The speaker in her helmet starts to crackle again.

"*MACY, CAN YOU HEAR ME?*" *EJ yells, gulping down the knot in her throat.* "*Please copy. Over.*"

EJ strains to hear the quiet sounds coming from the speaker: "*Dilemma Green! Gremlin Bean!*"

These words mean nothing to EJ. Then a thought crosses her mind: what if aliens have taken over the shuttle, are holding Macy hostage, and this is their bizarre language?

"*What DO YOU WANT?*" *EJ shouts into the helmet radio.*

"Emma Jean! Eeeee-Jaaaaay Payne!"

EJ snapped her head down to see Ms. Pickerington standing on the ground with a *very* unhappy look on her face. She realized she was no longer hanging a few feet from the ground, but was standing on top of the monkey-bar rungs, her hands outstretched into the sky as if she really were floating in space.

"Sit down, NOW!" Ms. Pickerington's face was getting redder with every syllable she shouted. Macy stood next to her, looking terrified.

EJ dropped to her knees and grabbed hold of the monkey-bar handles to steady herself before climbing down. *Oh no. . .EJ, you've really done it now,* she thought to herself.

"You could've fallen and split your head open!" Ms. P gasped at EJ, the teacher's hands firmly on EJ's shoulders as if she were keeping her from floating into space again. "Didn't you hear me yelling your name?"

"I. . .uh. . ." EJ stammered, looking down at her toes. "I thought you were an alien talking to me."

Ms. P's face went white, but was there a hint of amusement? "Emma Jean Payne, you've got to get your head out of the clouds," she said. "Figuratively *and* literally!"

Chapter 4

FAMILY CAMP

Dear Diary,

Family camp is here! Mom and Dad are downstairs packing the minivan for a Labor Day weekend of fun at Camp Christian. Camp Christian is a place where many of us Spooner kids spend part of our summer—church camp, basketball camp, soccer camp, music camp, theater camp; they even have a BMX camp. We sleep on creaky bunk beds in the dorms, do lots of great outdoor activities, make amazing crafts, and have fun Bible classes and worship services. Family camp is kind of like summer camp, except it's for moms and dads, too! Families pitch tents and set up fire pits and play board games, eat food (Mom makes an amazing apple turnover in the pie iron over the campfire), and share laughs. And there are so many fun things to do all weekend long: basketball, volleyball, fishing, biking. I'm most excited about swimming in the lake and trying out the diving ring set that I got for my birthday in June. They're weighted plastic rings that sink to the bottom, and you have to swim down to get them. I used them over the summer at the public pool, but when you're swimming in crystal-clear water, it's not much of a challenge. In a lake, it might be more like diving for treasure!

Isaac and I have our very own pup tents this year—mine looks like an actual puppy, with floppy ears on the sides; little round, mesh windows that look like eyes; and an opening that looks like the dog's mouth—complete with a zipper pull that looks like a red tongue! The Space Invader picked one that looks like a spider—a tiny round tent with eight tent poles that look like hairy arachnid legs and a dozen mesh window eyes on the top of the spider's head. It's a pretty cool tent, but not what I would've picked. And if that thing attracts creepy-crawlies to our campsite, I will not be okay with that.

Speaking of bugs, that reminds me—I need to go pack my bug spray. Talk to you later, Diary!

EJ

Saturday morning of family camp, EJ and Isaac were up with the break of dawn, ready to enjoy one of the last warm weekends of the year before the frigid, snowy Wisconsin winter set in. The Paynes' three-tent campsite also included a picnic table, fire ring, four lawn chairs (two adult-size and two kid-size), and Dad's hammock stretched between two nearby trees.

EJ helped fix breakfast (scrambled eggs and sausage links) by cracking six eggs in a plastic bowl and adding some milk, salt, and pepper. Then she beat the mixture with a whisk until they were light colored and frothy.

"The fire's just about right to start the sizzlin'," Dad called from the fire ring where he had stoked the fire, set up a grate, and placed a cast-iron frying pan over the hottest part of flame. Mom took the eggs and sausage over to Dad, who dumped everything into the pan. "Camp vittles don't look purdy, ma'am." Dad tipped his baseball cap like it was a ten-gallon hat, doing his best cowboy impression. "But it sure do taste good!"

Mom and EJ laughed. But just then they realized they were missing a distinct little boy laugh at their campsite.

"Where's Isaac?" Mom wondered out loud.

"I just saw him a few minutes ago out here playing with Bert," Dad said, looking around. "But here's Bert and no Isaac." Dad picked up the dog who was hopping a little too close to the fire, trying to sneak a taste of the sizzling sausage.

"Never fear, Isaac's here!" Isaac said as he popped out of his spider tent and struck a Superman-like pose. Except instead of tights and a cape, he was wearing his swim trunks, shark-fin floater vest, and goggles. "Let's go swimming!"

"Uh, Isaac. . .it's 9 a.m.," EJ said, while Mom and Dad laughed. "Swimming doesn't start till one o'clock."

"Oh." Isaac looked disappointed.

"Isaac, you can keep your trunks on so you're ready at one," Mom said. "Just go take off the shark fin for now and put on a shirt, okay?"

"Okay!" Isaac turned and dived back in his tent to change, but then had a second thought and poked his head out of the opening. "Marmalade?"

"What, buddy?" Mom didn't look up from the plastic box she was digging through to find plates and forks for breakfast.

"Can I leave my goggles on?" Isaac asked. "They help me see better."

EJ rolled her eyes.

"Sure, Isaac," Mom said. "That'll be fine."

The Paynes were just finished cleaning up from breakfast when Macy's bike screeched to a halt at the edge of their campsite.

"Hey, Mace!" EJ greeted her best friend happily. "What's up?"

"Well, I heard that the fish are biting this morning," Macy said, holding her junior-sized fishing pole across the handlebars of her bike. "And I wondered if you want to grab your pole and go to the lake with me."

"Yeah! Sure! Except. . ." EJ trailed off and added quietly, "I don't really want to touch worms. Or the fish for that matter."

"Oh, don't worry. I don't want to touch them either," Macy reassured EJ. "Bryan is down at the dock with a couple of his friends, and they'll do all the disgusting work for us." Bryan was Macy's fourteen-year-old brother, and as annoying as older brothers might be, at least they were good for touching gross things.

"Mom, can I go?" EJ looked hopefully at Mom.

"You may," Mom said, picking up a book from a lawn chair. "Just be back in time for lunch. I'll be reading in the hammock if you need me."

"I'm gonna catch the biggest fish in the history of fish!" Isaac showed up out of nowhere next to EJ, his tiny fishing pole in hand.

"You're not invited," EJ said as she swung a leg over her bike and adjusted her own pole across the handlebars. "Get lost, Space Invader."

"EJ, settle down," Dad said, giving her a warning look. "Isaac and I will come down a little later and catch that biggest fish in the history of fish." Then he added with a smile, "That is, unless Macy and EJ catch it first."

"We'll try, Mr. Payne," Macy called as she and EJ coasted away on their bikes.

"We just won't touch it!" EJ added over her shoulder.

The unsuccessful fishing trip started with Bryan helping the girls bait their hooks, but then he left with his friends three minutes later, leaving EJ and Macy alone on the fishing dock, each afraid that she would catch a fish and not know what to do with it. Thankfully, their worms fell off the hooks a short while later, so they just decided to go swing on the swing set until lunch. After a hot-dogs-roasted-over-the-fire lunch, the Paynes headed down to the waterfront for some swimming and boating.

Unfortunately, the diving rings were nothing like the high-seas adventure treasure hunt EJ had hoped for. Mom tossed the rings into the shallow water, and EJ and Isaac scrambled to find them, but there were so many kids churning up the murky lake water that twenty-five minutes later, they had only found the yellow one. Five other rings were somewhere at the bottom of the lake, buried under the sand.

"I'm sure we'll find the others once some of the swimmers clear out," Mom said.

"They're gone forever." EJ sighed.

Toweling off for a rest, EJ sat on the shore and looked around the waterfront: dozens of kids splashed happily in the shallow water. A few little kids played on the beach with sand toys and Hula-Hoops. Some teens were holding a diving contest on the high dive at the end of a wooden dock that jutted out into the deep water. A dark-haired college-aged lifeguard perched high on her chair held a red life-saving float across her knees as she took in the scene behind her sunglasses, making sure everyone was safe. And several parents sat on the grassy hillside that overlooked the swimming area, chatting and keeping half an eye on their kids in the water.

The scene seemed somehow familiar to her. . . .

"Marine World would like to introduce our newest staffer—dolphin trainer EJ Payne!" the announcer's voice echoes through the aquatic center. "EJ holds a degree in dolphinology from the world-famous Jacques Cousteau University and has spent the past year traveling around the world to study our underwater mammal friends. Please give a warm welcome to EJ!"

EJ steps out onto the deck, ready to soak in the audience's adoring applause. The people in the stands clap halfheartedly. Most aren't even looking at her.

Not to be so easily disappointed, EJ decides to give the audience a show unlike they've ever seen. She zips up her wet suit and slips a whistle around her neck before jumping into the shallow water.

Three short tweets on the whistle, and her very best dolphin performer, a young male named Squirt, is at her side, eager to get the show started.

"EJ and Squirt have been performing together since he was just a baby calf, ladies and gentlemen," the announcer says. "Watch as EJ cues Squirt with their special language."

EJ pats Squirt on the head and starts talking to him in short

*squeaks and clicks. Squirt waves a fin in the air, signaling that
he understands. The dolphin dives under the surface of the water.
Suddenly he bursts out of the water in a magnificent splash and slides
on his belly up on the pool deck.*

*The audience isn't impressed. A couple of them actually get up to
leave.*

*EJ scratches her head, trying to think of something that will excite
the crowd. She squeaks another command to Squirt, who shimmies
back into the water and makes another lap around the pool, this time
waving his tail back and forth as he passes the crowd. A few people
smile and clap. The next time around, he sprays a fine mist of water at
the crowd and gets a little more applause.*

Now they're warming up, *EJ thinks to herself.* Time to pull out
the big guns. *She cues Squirt for his next trick and picks up a large
plastic hoop from the deck.*

*EJ stands in her place and steadies the hoop, the bottom half down
in the water. She whistles a single tweet, and Squirt swims toward her,
right through the hoop.*

The audience seems bored again. All according to plan, *EJ thinks.*

*She raises the hoop so the bottom is just touching the surface of the
water and whistles two short tweets. Squirt swims a little faster and
bunny-hops through the hoop.*

The crowd perks up, and a few people clap.

*EJ raises the hoop higher off the water. Three tweets. Squirt
expertly jumps through and gives an extra tail wave at the end of the
jump. The crowd laughs and applauds.*

Now for the big finish, *EJ thinks. She gives Squirt a pat of
encouragement on his nose as he circles around. EJ holds the hoop in
position, outstretched over her head. Four tweets and she shuts her eyes
as Squirt gains speed, swimming right toward her. . .*

"Help! *(cough, splutter)* Help me!"

"Stop, Squirt. . .er. . .Isaac!" EJ put her hand out to stop Isaac from trying to jump through the hoop. "Someone needs help. . . ." EJ quickly saw Katy McCallister floundering in knee-deep shallow water a few feet away, gasping for breath. "Katy!" EJ yelled, grabbing Katy's small arm and pulling her up until she could get her footing on the lake bottom.

"Are you okay?" she asked a few moments later.

"Ye–yes, I'm okay," Katy said, still trying to catch her breath as EJ helped her to the shoreline. "I was trying to climb on an inflatable raft so I could watch you and Isaac play dolphin, and I slipped."

A few seconds later, Mrs. McCallister ran up to the girls.

"Oh, Katy, darling!" Mrs. McCallister gushed, wrapping Katy up in a towel. "I took my eyes off you for three seconds. . .three seconds! I told you the dirty lake is no place for a young lady to go swimming, but you insisted on it. . . ." Then she turned to EJ and said, "EJ, thank you for keeping an eye out for my little princess."

EJ wasn't about to tell Mrs. McCallister that Katy's shouting interrupted one of her daydreams and that was the only thing that snapped her out of it.

"It's no problem, Mrs. McCallister," EJ said.

"Next time maybe I can be a dolphin, too." Katy grinned at Isaac, who stood a few feet away taking in the whole scene silently.

"Sure. Next time." EJ laughed to herself. Maybe Katy wasn't so bad—even if CoraLee *was* her older sister.

"What are you talking about, Katy? Dolphin? . . ." Mrs. McCallister asked Katy as they walked away, hand in hand.

"Come on, Squirt." EJ stepped toward the water and motioned for Isaac to follow her. "We've still got the big jump to do!"

Chapter 5

JUST A LITTLE OFF THE TOP

September 14

Dear Diary,

I've told you before that my hair is basically a tragedy. Well, it's about to get even more tragic because Mom just told me we're leaving in a few minutes to go get haircuts. This isn't going to end well, Diary.

My bangs are finally recovering from the last hatchet job Mom did on them a couple of weeks ago. I've been very careful not to let the bangs get anywhere near my eyes so she doesn't have an excuse to cut them again. Now, you might be thinking that having a professional fix me up would help my sad hair situation, but Mom gives the beautician very specific ideas about how she wants my hair to be cut: trimmed just above my shoulders and bangs just long enough that they barely lay down on my forehead. One of my bangs massacres crossed the line of too short, and I had to endure a week of bangs that stood straight up all the way across my forehead. Thankfully, Mom let me wear hats as much as possible that week. And when I couldn't wear a hat, I wore a wide headband to cover up the sad state of my head. (I think Mom felt worse than me that time.)

Anyway, Diary, Mom's taking me to a new hairdresser, and she promises that I'll like this one. We'll see. I guess she couldn't really make my hair any worse than it already is.

Here goes nothing.

Tragic-haired EJ

EJ sat in a molded plastic chair in the waiting area of Cuts-4-Less, flipping through a book of hairstyles and getting more and more disappointed in her own hair.

"Look at this one, Mom." EJ pointed to a short bob that flipped out—and the best part: side-swooped bangs. "It's sort of like Macy's, but bouncier." She imagined the two of them together with their cute, sassy hairstyles.

"EJ, we've been over this." Mom looked up from the papers she was grading and stuck the red pen in her hair until she was ready for it again. "You like wearing your hair in a ponytail, remember? Until you decide that you want to fix your hair every day, we have to keep it long enough to pull back—"

"—because it is a stringy mess if I don't do anything to it," EJ finished Mom's thought. "I know. I hate my hair."

Mom cleared her throat and raised a warning eyebrow at EJ.

"I *strongly dislike* my hair." EJ corrected her use of *hate,* a word that Mom *strongly disliked.*

EJ hid behind the hairstyle book again, imagining anything better than the sadness that was currently on top of her head.

"EJ?" said a friendly voice from the other side of the book. "I'm ready for you."

EJ shut the hairstyle book and placed it back on the table with the others before looking up to see a young hairstylist smiling at her. Short and spunky, the hairstylist looked like she was just out of beauty college. She wore black ballet flats, black skinny jeans, and a short-sleeved black cardigan—but underneath the cardigan was a sequined red-and-pink shirt that shimmered when it caught the light. Her fingernails were each painted a different color, and her eye shadow had just the right amount of sparkle in it. Her jet-black hair was pulled back into two intricate french braids and her bangs—well, her bangs were as painfully short as EJ's. Except on this girl,

EJ thought they looked absolutely cool.

"Right this way," the girl said, ushering EJ to her chair in the far corner of the salon. "I'm Ashley, by the way."

"I'm EJ," EJ said, getting comfortable in the chair as Ashley turned it so EJ faced the mirror.

"EJ, right on—nice to meet you!" Ashley said, standing behind EJ and smiling at her in the mirror. "What are we doing to your beautiful hair today?"

EJ laughed and said, "Beautiful hair? Who are you looking at?" She pulled the ponytail holder out of her hair so Ashley could get a good look at what she was dealing with. "It's a tragedy."

"Oh no, I wouldn't say *that*." Ashley combed through EJ's hair with her fingers. "What don't you like about it?"

EJ counted on her fingers as she went through the list. "The color, the length, the texture, and the bangs are the worst," she said. "Your bangs are short, and they look so nice. And your hair is such a great color. And your clothes and makeup are all amazing!"

Realizing she was gushing at someone she had just met, EJ sat back in the chair and added, "I guess we're not all meant to be beautiful."

"Whoa, take a breather there, EJ," Ashley said. "You think all of this just happens? No, my friend, this is W-O-R-K." Ashley pointed to her hair. "My natural color? Brown. But not the pretty kind—the kind that looks like it was left out in the rain. Nothing a little hair dye can't fix. My hair's natural texture? Curly with a nice side of frizz. Had to invest in a high-quality straightener."

"I guess that's why Mom wants to keep my hair low-maintenance while I'm a kid," EJ said. "And she says I'm not allowed to wear makeup till I'm thirty-five."

"Here's a little tip from a pro, EJ," Ashley said, smiling. "Stay a kid as long as you can. The hair and makeup will wait. And

DIARY OF A REAL PAYNE: TRUE STORY

anyway, true beauty isn't on the outside anyway."

Mom had always said that what was on the inside is more important that what the outside looks like—but EJ knew that's what moms are supposed to say. EJ was surprised to hear similar words coming out of Ashley's mouth.

"Be a good friend," Ashley said. "Be nice to babies, animals, and old people, and treat others the way you want to be treated. That's what makes a person beautiful. Now, I have a couple ideas for your hair. . . ."

Ashley brought Mom over for a quick conference to discuss how she was going to cut EJ's hair, and Mom gave her blessing. Ashley turned EJ away from the mirror so she couldn't see what was happening to her hair and set to work.

Soon the hair started flying, all the while Ashley and EJ chatted about this and that. EJ found out that Ashley had a brother who was five years younger than her. "Oh, EJ, he annoyed me to death when we were kids!" Ashley said. "But not very long ago I realized he wasn't just an annoying little brother to me. . .he's my friend, too."

A few minutes later, Ashley announced "Finished!" and twirled the chair around so EJ could see her brand-new look in the mirror. EJ's jaw dropped.

Looking back at her was a girl with an adorable layered haircut that worked just perfectly with her sort-of curly hair. Where it wanted to flip, the layers allowed it to flip. And where it wanted to lay flat, it could be straight. The layers let the natural highlights (the blond) and lowlights (the brown) of her hair shine through. Her bangs were cut shorter than they'd ever been cut, but instead of looking like it was a mistake, they looked like they came straight from the pages of the hairstyle books in the waiting area.

"Woo–oow!" EJ said as she admired Ashley's work in the mirror. She wondered if those scissors didn't have a little bit of magic in them. "I *love* it!"

"I'll show you a couple quick tips for when you want to wear it down," Ashley said, picking up a round brush. "Who knows? Maybe hairstyling is in your future."

★

EJ flips the sign on the salon's front door from CLOSED *to* OPEN. *Her first client of the day will arrive any moment, but she takes the time to straighten the sign behind her workstation:* SUPER STYLZ SALON. *After studying hairstyling at the world-famous Hair Parfaite Beauty College in Paris, she has just opened her first salon in New York City and is already booking celebrities.*

She's a trendsetter and a style expert with her perfect hair, clothes, makeup, and accessories. She must look the part if she wants to keep her clients. EJ sits for a moment, calmly sipping a mocha cappuccino. She leans down to pet her stylish pooch, Bert, who is sitting under her hairdresser chair, gnawing at his blue rhinestone collar.

The door opens, and the bell hanging at the top announces a client's arrival.

"Ah, mon cheri! *Welcome!" EJ still holds on to the bizarre French accent she picked up in Paris. "Come. . .seet."*

"Uh. . .EJ?" Isaac peeked through EJ's bedroom door with a confused expression. "Do you want to play checkers?"

"Monsiour Trump, you are just een time for your haircut." EJ motions for the millionaire business mogul to sit in the chair. "Now ees no time for games!"

"Why are you talking like that?" Isaac asked, still confused. "And who is Mr. Trump?"

"Isaac!" EJ said, exasperated. "I'm a world-famous hairstylist, and you're my high-profile client, Donald Trump. You in or out?"

"Oh! In!" Isaac immediately got into character by scrunching up his face and doing his best impression of the famous rich guy.

"EJ, I'm ready for a change," Mr. Trump says as he sits in the swivel chair. "The public seems to think that I wear a toupee, so I think it's time I get a haircut that proves them wrong."

"You haf come to zee right place, Mr. Trump," EJ replies. "Shall I, as you Americans say, 'take a little off zee top'?"

"Weren't you born in Kentucky?" Mr. Trump asks, looking suspicious.

"Oh, yes—you're right!" EJ responds, dropping the accent. "Don't worry, Mr. Trump. You're in good hands."

The two chat while EJ snaps a hairdresser cape around his neck and begins to work.

"So, do you have any new hotels opening soon?" EJ asks, snipping away.

"Yes—one I'm very excited about!" Mr. Trump says. "It's a hotel that will be staffed entirely by robot dinosaurs."

"Sounds. . .interesting." EJ looks skeptical, her scissors still cutting. "Will the robots be friendly, or will they want to eat the guests?"

"Most will be friendly," Mr. Trump explains. "But if someone leaves a room in a terrible mess, the housekeeping dinosaurs have been known to hunt down a guest and bite off an arm."

"You might have a problem getting repeat customers," EJ says, glancing down at her masterpiece.

Staring back at her is a quarter-sized bald spot on the back of Isaac's head.

"Don't panic, Isaac," she said, grabbing his shoulders.

"Wait, I thought I was Donald Trump!" Isaac said, turning to look at EJ. When he saw the look in her eyes, he got nervous. "What'd you do?"

Isaac reached up quickly, patting his head all over. "You weren't really cutting my hair, were you? We were just pretending, EJ!"

"I guess I got a little carried away." EJ bent down and picked up the chunk of hair that was on the floor. She tried to pat it into place over the bald spot. But it immediately fell on the floor again. The two stared at the ball of hair and then at each other.

"Mom's gonna kill us." Isaac groaned, covering his bald spot with his hand.

EJ's brain whirred. She knew she'd get another lecture about being aware of her surroundings if Mom and Dad saw Isaac's bald spot. The truth was, she *had* been doing a little better. Didn't she snap out of her daydream when she heard Katy McCallister yelling for help at family camp? This time. . .well, this time she was back to her old ways, and poor Isaac was suffering the consequences.

"Listen, Isaac, neither of us wants to get into trouble," EJ said, doing her best to comb a couple of Isaac's curls over the bald spot. "How would you feel about wearing hats for the next few weeks?"

"I *love* hats," Isaac responded. "Hats are my favorite."

Chapter 6

THE SPELLING BEE(KEEPER)

September 26

Dear Diary,

Other than reading, my favorite (and best) subject in school is S-P-E-L-L-I-N-G. In third grade I went sixteen weeks of the school year without missing a single word on a spelling test. And it was only a completely tricky word like avocado that tricked me on week seventeen. (Personally, I think the word should be spelled A-V-A-C-A-D-O, just like it sounds. I wrote a letter to Mr. Merriam and Mr. Webster, asking them to consider changing the spelling of the word. I'm expecting a response any day now.)

Tomorrow is the fourth-grade spelling bee at Spooner Elementary, and I am absolutely ready to dominate, Diary. I think my biggest competition is going to be CoraLee McCallister, but I know if I try my hardest, I can win.

Do you know why a spelling competition is called a bee? I didn't know either, but I looked it up: bee refers to a gathering where friends and neighbors join together

in a single activity (like sewing, quilting, barn raising, etc.).
People started using the word *bee* because the events
reminded them of the organized crowds of bees in a
beehive.

It's about time for bed, but I think I'll go get the *B*
encyclopedia from Dad's bookshelf and read a little bit
about bees, beehives, honey, and beekeepers. This might be
another career to consider. . . .

EJ

EJ held her hand out, palm up, and imagined a honeybee landing on her fingertip and walking up her pointer finger toward her palm.

"Hey there, little guy," she whispered to the imaginary bee. "We're doing a spelling one of you today."

"Who are you talking to?" CoraLee whispered sharply from her desk across the aisle. "Pay attention—Ms. P is giving instructions."

EJ made a face at CoraLee and allowed the imaginary bee to fly away before turning her attention to Ms. Pickerington at the front of the classroom.

"Students who have qualified for the spelling bee will come and line up at the door," Ms. Pickerington said. "Once you arrive at the gymnasium, you will be seated in alphabetical order by last name. Everyone else will sit in the audience."

EJ, CoraLee, and about a dozen other students from their class lined up at the door.

"CoraLee, please lead the line *quietly* through the hallway to the gym," Ms. Pickerington said. "I'll follow behind with the rest of the class."

"Yes, Ms. P." CoraLee gave EJ a smug smile and stepped to the front of the line.

When they arrived at the gymnasium doors, a sixth-grader named Kelsey was there to make sure they got to the correct seats on the stage.

"CoraLee McCallister—here." Kelsey pointed at an empty chair while checking the clipboard she had in her hand. "Emma Jean Payne—here."

"Great." EJ sighed and reluctantly slid into the chair next to CoraLee.

A few seats down the row, Macy took her spot at the end of the *R*s after Kurt Roberts and flashed EJ a thumbs-up sign. EJ smiled and waved, wishing she were sitting next to Macy instead of CoraLee.

"Good luck. You'll need it." CoraLee crossed her arms and turned away from EJ.

"Thanks," EJ said.

⭐

EJ felt the knot in her stomach tighten as the spelling bee started. It helped to see Dad's friendly face in the third row (Mom was sitting with her second graders in the bleachers), but she wanted so badly to win that her nerves were wound tight. Plus, as a *P* name, she had to wait through all of the *A*s and up through CoraLee McCallister—at least half an eternity.

"Aardvark," Betsy Dillon recited. "A-R-R-D-V-A-R-K. Aardvark."

Ding, went the bell.

"I'm sorry, that is incorrect," said Mrs. McIntosh, the school librarian and spelling bee judge. "The correct spelling of aardvark is A-A-R-D-V-A-R-K."

Betsy hung her head and walked off the stage.

"Heh. Rookie mistake," CoraLee whispered, rolling her eyes.

EJ couldn't take much more of CoraLee's running commentary, and if she didn't find a way to relax before it was her turn, she was afraid her peanut butter and banana sandwich might make a reappearance. So she sat back and closed her eyes and thought back to the encyclopedia entry about beekeeping she'd read the night before.

EJ pulls down the netting of her beekeeper helmet so that her face and neck are protected from the thousands of honeybees buzzing in the gymnasium. Nobody else can see the bees, but to EJ, they're real. She

raises her hand to eye level to admire the dozens of tiny fuzzy bodies
that are swarmed on her protective glove.

"Hey, you bees, I'm not paying you to sit around," she says to the
bees and smiles. "Go make some honey!" With her other hand, she
pumps a contraption that looks a little like a tall silver teapot with a
small accordion attached to the back, until smoke streams out of the
spout that gently shoos the bees away from her glove.

Seeing the empty seat next to her, EJ realized CoraLee was
already up at the mic stand, spelling her first word.

"Fleece," CoraLee recited before spelling confidently, "F-L-E-
E-C-E. Fleece."

"Correct," Mrs. McIntosh said.

CoraLee walked back to her seat, nose in the air. EJ tried not
to look at her as she walked to the mic.

"EJ, your word is *relevant*," Mrs. McIntosh said.

EJ took a deep breath and looked out at the many eyeballs
staring back at her before speaking into the mic. "Relevant. May I
have the definition?"

"Something that is relevant is closely connected or appropriate
to the matter at hand," Mrs. McIntosh read from the book in front
of her.

EJ's ears started buzzing.

EJ looks up to see a cloud of honeybees a few feet above her head.
"Come on, guys, I can't concentrate—" she starts.

But then a memory flashes across her mind. Relevant is the name
of a magazine that Mom and Dad read. She squints, trying to visualize
what the word looks like on the cover. Suddenly the swarm of bees starts
to form the letters of the word in front of her: R-e-l. . .

"Relevant," EJ said as she snapped out of her daydream. "R-E-
L-E-V-A-N-T. Relevant!"

"Correct," Mrs. McIntosh said.

☆

Much to EJ's disappointment, Macy went out in round two when she put one too many *na*'s in bandana. But by round four, EJ was still going strong after correctly spelling *laughter, forecast*, and *embarrass*. CoraLee was also still in it, spelling *beautiful, together*, and *voyage* correctly. Starting round five, the only other person left was Krista Kelly, a bubbly redhead who everybody called Krista K.

The pressure must've gotten to Krista K at round five when she spelled bureau, B-E-U-R-O. *Ding*, went the bell, and Krista K's face turned as red as her hair.

"Good try. That's a hard one," EJ whispered to Krista K as the audience clapped her off the stage.

With just two spellers left, they automatically moved on to round six. Mrs. McIntosh called for a two-minute break while the sixth graders removed all the chairs from the stage except two for EJ and CoraLee.

"Girls!" Ms. Pickerington called as she rushed across the stage. "You both are doing simply wonderfully! You will represent our class so well—great job!"

"Thanks, Ms. P!" EJ smiled, thinking how nice it felt to be on her teacher's good side.

"Some of us have gotten easier words than others," CoraLee said coldly.

"I'm proud of both of you," Ms. Pickerington said, ignoring CoraLee's comment.

As the audience settled down for the beginning of the next round, CoraLee turned to EJ and looked her straight in the eye.

"Just so you know, Payne-in-my-neck," CoraLee hissed, "Katy told me all about your little dolphin trainer daydream at family camp. For some dumb reason, she thinks you are so cool and she wants to be just like you."

EJ smiled to herself. She knew she liked Katy.

"Well, I know what you *really* are." CoraLee took a deep breath. "You're nothing but a girl who knows she'll never do anything important, so she has to *imagine* that she's better than everyone else."

"It's time to start round six," Mrs. McIntosh announced into the microphone.

EJ stared at CoraLee, speechless that she could be so mean.

"EJ, your word is *misspell*," Mrs. McIntosh said.

EJ blinked and walked up to the mic stand. "I'm sorry. Would you repeat the word, please?"

"Misspell," the librarian said again.

EJ shook her head to try to clear CoraLee's words that were shouting on repeat:

"Never do anything important. . ."

"Has to imagine *that she's better than everyone else. . ."*

EJ smoothes the cuffs of her protective gloves and adjusts her beekeeper helmet. She glances up to find that her swarm of bee friends are missing. There's no reassuring buzzing sound—just silence. She looks down and sees a single honeybee sitting on the microphone in front of her. She can't see the word.

"Misspell. M-I-S. . ." EJ hesitated. ". . .P-E-L-L?"

Ding. "Incorrect."

EJ's brain explodes. Two *s*'s! She knew it! Why had she let CoraLee get into her head like that?

EJ slouched and stood back from the mic. There was still hope—CoraLee would have to correctly spell EJ's word *plus* another word.

CoraLee took her spot behind the mic and barked out, "Misspell. M-I-S-S- (of course she just *had* to put the emphasis on the second *s*) P-E-L-L. Misspell."

"Correct," Mrs. McIntosh said. "CoraLee, your final word is *definitely*."

"Definitely. D-E—" CoraLee started.

Just one letter wrong. Come on, CoraLee, you want to put an a in there somewhere, EJ silently wished.

"—F-I-N-I-T-E-L-Y. Definitely!"

"You *definitely* know how to spell that word," Mrs. McIntosh said. "Congratulations to CoraLee McCallister, this year's fourth-grade spelling champion!"

The audience burst into applause. CoraLee squealed and jumped up and down, making the ruffles on her purple skirt bounce. EJ clapped halfheartedly, trying not to look as utterly miserable as she felt.

⭐

The Paynes stopped for ice cream on the way home—celebratory cones for EJ's second-place finish in the spelling bee, Dad said. EJ couldn't help but think that her soft-serve twist cone with rainbow sprinkles would've tasted a lot better if she'd won.

"You know why my kids are so amazing?" Dad mused as they sat at a picnic table outside the Spooner Dari-Bar. "Because they got the brains *and* good looks from their mom!"

"And from their dad they got their winning personalities and the wittiest senses of humor," Mom said, kissing Dad on the cheek between bites of vanilla ice cream.

Isaac covered his eyes with his hand not holding a cone.

"Gross." EJ rolled her eyes and concentrated on licking sprinkles off her ice cream cone.

"EJ, I was really impressed with the words you spelled today," Mom said. "*Embarrass* is one of those words I have to stop and think every time I spell it—how many *m*'s, *r*'s and *s*'s are in it."

"Thanks, except I was really *embarrassed* when the word I misspelled to go out was *misspell*," EJ said grumpily. "What a waste."

"A waste? I don't think so!" Dad said, crunching on the last bit of his waffle cone. "Anyway, you'll have plenty of time to study between now and the district spelling bee in the spring."

"Why would I study for the district spelling bee?" EJ asked. "*I didn't win*, remember?"

"The top three spellers advance to the district bee, EJ," Mom said. "Ms. P didn't tell you that?"

"No, she didn't." EJ replayed the conversation with Ms. Pickerington on the stage before round six. "*You will represent our class so well*". . .in the district spelling bee must've been what she meant!

"All right, EJ! Cool!" Isaac got up from his seat and ran to EJ, holding up his melted ice-cream-drenched hand for a high five.

Before EJ could slap her hand against his (just this once—she *was* pretty excited about the district bee), Mom exclaimed, "ISAAC DAVID PAYNE! Did you cut your hair?"

Isaac had been so careful since the hair-cutting incident to comb his curls to cover up the bald spot, to wear baseball hats whenever he could, and most importantly, to not turn his back toward Mom. But in this moment of excitement, he had forgotten about all three of those things.

"Umm." Isaac gave EJ a panicked look as Mom hovered over

Isaac, parting his hair with her hands so she could get a good look at the damage.

"I did it," EJ admitted. "I was a hairstylist and Isaac was my client, and well. . .it got a little too real, a little too fast."

"Oh, EJ," Mom said. "When will you *learn*?"

"Mom, don't worry. Hair is the one part of me that is like a lizard's tail," Isaac said—as if he'd been saving this statement to diffuse the situation. "Cut it off, and it will grow back!"

Chapter 7

THE PAYNE-FULLY SPECTACULAR CIRCUS

Dear Diary,

A couple of weeks ago, Dad told me about a circus he went to when he was a kid. I've only seen a circus on TV or in a movie, but when Dad was explaining what an actual circus is like, it made me want to see one in real life! The excitement of the crowd, the bright colors of the costumes, the ringmaster and his (or her) powerful voice, the music of the band as each act is introduced, the exotic animals and their tricks, the high-wire acts, even the silliness of the clowns.

The next day at school, Ms. P announced that the annual holiday Spooner Elementary food drive would begin the second week in October, so we should start collecting canned and boxed foods from home and friends and neighbors. This gave me a great idea! What if I organized a traveling circus act to go door-to-door in my neighborhood to ask for food donations in exchange for a show? There's no way people would say no to that! (Right?)

Macy's coming over tomorrow morning, and the Space Invader has a friend named Bruce coming over, too, so they'll both be part of the circus act. And Bert's always ready to perform his favorite tricks—especially when he knows there are treats involved.

I'd better go work on my ringmaster voice!

EJ

EJ rolled up the sleeves of Dad's old sport jacket (a substitute tailcoat for her ringmaster costume) and adjusted the top hat she had fashioned out of an empty oatmeal container. She stood in the driveway next to a little red wagon, a hand-painted sign hanging from the side that said:

THE PAYNE-FULLY SPECTACULAR CIRCUS
(DONATIONS FOR THE SPOONER ELEMENTARY
FOOD DRIVE ACCEPTED)

Bert sat happily in the empty wagon, wearing a pointy hat, a red clown nose, and a collar EJ had made out of coffee filters, folded fan-style. Macy stood a few feet away in a silver gymnast leotard and warm-up pants, stretching her legs and arms in preparation for her debut as the circus acrobat.

"Let's go, boys!" EJ hollered. "Mom says we have to be back in time for lunch!"

Isaac rounded the side of the house a few moments later, running at top speed toward EJ and the wagon. His costume was made up of a pair of red galoshes, dinosaur swim trunks, a Green Bay Packers long-sleeved T-shirt, a blue handkerchief tied around his head, and for extra flair, the cape from his Superman pajamas.

"What's he supposed to be?" Macy asked, giving Isaac a wary look. Little brothers were a mystery to Macy.

"He's an animal trainer," EJ answered, not fazed a bit by Isaac's bizarre costume. At least he had a shirt on this time. "What animal did you decide you were going to tame, Isaac?"

Isaac grinned and pointed back the way he had just come. EJ and Macy laughed at what they saw: a chubby kindergartener-sized body with the head of a Tyrannosaurus Rex walked slowly toward them, arms outstretched, zombie-like. Seeing that Bruce was having some difficulty, Isaac skipped over to him, grabbed him by the hand, and led him to where EJ and Macy stood. Bert barked, hopped out of the wagon, and sniffed at the dinosaur suspiciously.

Bruce pulled the flexible plastic mask off his head to reveal a red-faced little kid, his dark hair already sweaty and matted to his forehead. "It's hot in there, and I can't see too good," he huffed.

"Don't worry, it'll be great," Isaac said, patting his friend on the back.

"Everybody ready?" EJ glanced at the others. Their outfits looked pretty ridiculous (well, all except Macy's whose was an *actual* costume), but they'd done the best they could. "Let's go!"

Macy hit the Play button on the small CD player in the red wagon, and the performers marched down the sidewalk in time with the circus band music blaring from the speakers.

"Ladies and gentlemen! Boys and girls!" Ringmaster EJ uses her booming voice to start the show. She stands on a small stage, a bright spotlight drawing the audience's attention to only her. "Tonight we present to you three acts of circus entertainment at its finest. . . ."

The front door of the house opened, and the Paynes' neighbor, Mr. Hurdle, stuck his head out. Seeing four oddly dressed kids, a dog dressed as a clown, and the wagon, he smiled and turned his head back inside and called, "Honey, I think you're gonna want to see this." A few moments later, his very pregnant wife appeared in the door.

". . .So without any further ado—sit back, relax, and enjoy the Payne-fully Spectacular Ciiiiircuuuuus!" EJ removes her top hat and bows deeply, ushering on the first act as the audience applauds expectantly.

"First up: Macy the Magnificent!"

The music swells as the spotlight swerves to focus on acrobat Macy the Magnificent. She jumps and spins before starting into a routine that captivates the audience with her amazing abilities. Back bends, cartwheels, roundoffs, flips, and twists—the audience oohs and aahhs with each pass she makes.

"Ladies and gentlemen, as you hear the music build to the finale, Macy the Magnificent will attempt a new personal record of a full front flapjack with a double tuck and a triple twist!" EJ announces to the audience.

"EJ, those aren't real things," Macy whispered to EJ, looking nervous. "I don't know what you're talking about."

"Just do something that looks cool," EJ whispered back. "I'm improvising!"

Macy the Magnificent takes a deep breath and completes a perfectly executed string of back flips and twists that ends in full splits, Macy waving to the crowd.

The young couple clapped and whistled.

"Now, ladies and gentlemen, for your viewing pleasure—Bert the Boisterous!" Bert hops on his back legs into the spotlight and around in a tight circle as the audience claps their applause.

"Good dog. Sit," EJ commands, and Bert obeys. They run through his tricks: speak, lie down, play dead, and roll over. EJ rewards Bert with a treat she pulls from her pocket as the audience claps and cheers.

"Finally, from the wilds of Jurassic Park, the Payne-fully Spectacular Circus presents Impressive Isaac and his T-Rex!" EJ steps aside as Isaac leads his dinosaur into place.

"Rooooooooaaaaaaaaaaar!" the T-Rex screams, his tiny arms pawing at the air.

"Watch as Impressive Isaac shows you how he has tamed this deadly predator," EJ says, adding urgency to her voice to create a feeling of danger.

The music suddenly changed from marching band music to "The Hokey Pokey," and Isaac and Bruce followed the song's instructions, dancing and singing like it was a completely normal thing for a dinosaur and his trainer to do: "You put your left hand in, you put your left hand out. You put your left hand in, and you shake it all about. . . ." Mr. and Mrs. Hurdle burst into laughter.

EJ panicked and looked over at Macy, who was giggling at the sight of the chubby T-Rex "shaking it all about." Well, maybe it wasn't what EJ had in mind for the death-defying part of the act, but she had to admit it *was* entertaining.

The audience howls with laugher as "The Hokey Pokey" finishes up and Impressive Isaac and his T-Rex take a bow. EJ steps back into the spotlight.

"Ladies and gentlemen, we hope you enjoyed our little show for you today," EJ says, holding her top hat over her chest.

"If you liked what we did, would you consider donating some food to help us fill our wagon for the school food drive?" EJ asked, smiling her most convincing smile.

"Every little bit helps," Macy said, wheeling the wagon close to the front door.

"Rooooaaaar!" Bruce added.

"That means 'please,' " Isaac interpreted for the dinosaur.

A few minutes later, the couple handed over a shopping bag filled with two cans of green beans, a box of instant stuffing, and a plastic bottle of tomato juice. "Absolutely worth the price of admission to such a great show," Mrs. Hurdle said.

"Come again anytime," Mr. Hurdle added.

"Thank you!" the kids called as they headed down the driveway toward the next house. EJ pulled Bert in the wagon behind her.

"Only fourteen more houses to go to cover the neighborhood," EJ said. "You guys in?"

"The show must go on!" Macy said, turning a cartwheel.

"Leeet's do it!" Isaac jumped and pumped his fist in the air, his Superman cape fluttering behind him. "You okay in there, Bruce?"

"Yeah, I'm okay," Bruce's muffled voice said through the mask.

"I might need to stop for a juice box after the next house, though."

⭐

The next thirteen shows of the Payne-fully Spectacular Circus were so successful that they had to stop at home three times to empty the wagon and make room for more donations. Finally, they had just one more house in the neighborhood. . .but it was the house EJ and Isaac most wanted to avoid.

"It's Mr. Johnson's house," EJ explained to Macy and Bruce as they stood at the end of the driveway. "He's an old grump."

Mr. Johnson spent his days mowing his grass, trimming his shrubs and trees, and making sure nobody set foot on his property. The location of his house was a little unfortunate in this fact because every kid in the neighborhood had made the mistake (only once) of cutting through his yard to get to the playground that was on the other side of his property and through a little clump of trees.

"You get outta here!" EJ could remember the old man's gravelly voice yelling from the front porch like it was yesterday. *"This is my property, and you have no right to be here!"* His cat, named Gruff, was just as unpleasant as his owner and usually hissed at anyone who came too close to the yard.

"EJ, he can't be *that* bad," Macy said, taking a couple steps onto Mr. Johnson's driveway. "Anyway, it's for a good cause. Come on, what's the worst that could happen?"

EJ didn't want to think about what the worst could be. Maybe Mr. Johnson had a cage in his basement where he would lock up kids who didn't listen to his warnings to stay off his property. *No, that's silly*, EJ reasoned with herself. *That only happens in the movies.*

The circus troupe cautiously tiptoed up the driveway. When they got into place, EJ took a deep breath to calm her nerves then stepped up and knocked on the door.

"Ladies and gentlemen, boys and girls." *Ringmaster EJ starts her welcome, now perfectly timed after all the practice she's had in the earlier shows. "Tonight we present to you three acts of circus entertainment at its finest. . . ."*

The front door opened, and a wrinkled face with two bushy eyebrows peered out. Gruff the cat appeared around his ankles, looking annoyed and feisty.

"Who is it?" Mr. Johnson barked, squinting through the lenses of his glasses and leaning on the doorknob for support.

"M—Mr. Johnson, we're here to collect canned goods for the school food drive," EJ stammered, holding on to Bert's collar so he couldn't run after Gruff.

"Well, why are you dressed like idiots?" Mr. Johnson looked at the odd attire of the kids standing before him. Isaac sidestepped behind Bruce to hide.

"Sir, we're just trying to share a little entertainment with people who are donating food," Macy spoke clearly and respectfully, not seeming at all afraid of the man standing in front of them. "Would you like us to do our show for you?"

"No!" Mr. Johnson glared at Macy. "And I don't care to donate, either. Now get off my property before I call the police!" For added emphasis, Gruff hissed and streaked back into the house as Mr. Johnson slammed the door.

The kids looked at each other, disappointed and a little relieved all at the same time.

"That went well." EJ grimaced. "Let's get out of here and go home. Dad's making his famous grilled cheese and tomato soup for lunch."

Chapter 8

THE NOT-SO-STARRING ROLE

Dear Diary,

Tonight's the night I've been waiting for my whole life. Well, technically I've been waiting for tonight since ten days ago when Mom told me that the church is putting on a nativity pageant this Christmas. But I was born for this. And by this, I mean playing the part of Mary in the play.

Think of it, Diary: Mary, a young Jewish teenager living in small-town Israel (and let's be real... Nazareth was probably even more of a snoozefest than Spooner). Maybe Mary had exciting plans for herself when she grew up, or maybe not—but there's no way she could've guessed the big awesome amazing eternity-changing plans that God had in store when He chose her to be the mother of Jesus! Can you even imagine how shocking and scary and thrilling that must've been?

Mrs. Winkle is directing the nativity pageant, so I'm sure I'll get the part I want. But I'm not taking any chances—I've been working on my pregnant look by stuffing not one, but two couch pillows under my shirt for a nice nine-month-padded belly. Mom's impressed with my I'm-so-pregnant-I'm-about-to-pop-so-please-Joseph-find-a-place-for-us-to-stay groans and sighs. She says she should know a thing or two about being extra pregnant and uncomfortable because Isaac was born ten days after his due date.

Even in the womb the Space Invader was already a problem child.

Isaac told me he wants to be an elephant in the manger scene because elephants make the best noises in all of the animal kingdom. I told him he has boogers for brains and he'd better read his Bible again because there definitely weren't any elephants at the birth of Jesus. Maybe a goat. He could do an exceptionally good goat noise.

Wish me luck, Diary. Better yet, wish me a broken leg!

EJ

"Now, my dears, I don't want anyone to feel nervous that they won't get a part in the pageant."

Mrs. Winkle stood at the front of the church's auditorium in all her glory: yellow-and-black checkered pants, an orange sweater embroidered with pink flamingos, and a tiny Mexican sombrero perched on her head. EJ wasn't sure if the kids sitting in the pews looking up at Mrs. Winkle were actually listening to the words she was saying or if they were just dumbstruck by the outfit she was wearing.

"There are important parts for every single one of you at the nativity—it just takes a little creativity," Mrs. Winkle said, pointing a pen in the air for emphasis on the word *creativity.*

A couple of adult volunteers assisted Mrs. Winkle in splitting up the kids into age groups: preschool and kindergarten would be playing the part of animals, so they went to a room to practice animal noises and the songs they would sing; first through third grade would be the angel choir, so they went to another room to learn lines and songs; and the oldest kids in the pageant—the fourth graders—stayed with Mrs. Winkle in the auditorium to find out who would be playing which speaking roles in the pageant— Mary, Joseph, shepherds, wise men, and the angel.

EJ looked around at her competition for Mary: Sara Powers, who was at least a foot taller than any of the boys (*Mary can't be taller than Joseph,* EJ reasoned); Leslie Sattler who was so shy that the one time her mom made her sing in kids' choir at church, she stood onstage and sobbed the whole way through the song (EJ tried to imagine Leslie playing Mary, but all she could see was Leslie up onstage crying right along with the baby Jesus); and last (and in EJ's opinion, certainly least) CoraLee McCallister. EJ couldn't imagine CoraLee ever playing the role of the mother of Jesus—calm, gentle Mary, so full of beauty and kindness.

Mrs. Winkle read the cast list from her clipboard:
"Patrick Steiner, Wade Thompson, and Sara Powers will play
the roles of the three wise guys."

"Mrs. Winkle?" Sara asked, raising her hand. "I'm a girl. . . ."

"Indeed you are, Sara." Mrs. Winkle gave her a reassuring
smile. "We're taking a little creative license and calling them 'guys'
this year—two wise men and one wise woman!"

"Cool." Sara smiled and joined Patrick and Wade on the stage
where an adult volunteer named Mrs. Anderson searched through
a rack of clothes to fit each person with a costume.

"Our shepherds will be Nick Smith, Sam Duncan, Will
Bowers, and Cory Liden," Mrs. Winkle read off her list. The boys
hopped up onstage and formed a cluster, already planning how
they would keep their herd of sheep in order.

"I have a special behind-the-scenes role that I would like to
ask Leslie to fill this year," Mrs. Winkle said. She looked down at
Leslie, who was already on the verge of tears at the possibility that
she would be asked to go up onstage. "Leslie, how would you like
to be my assistant producer? No lines, no singing, no being in
front of people—just lots of work to help me make sure things are
going well behind the scenes."

"I—I think I could do that," Leslie whispered, breathing a sigh
of relief. Mrs. Winkle leaned down and gave her a quick hug.

"Now. . .let me see. . .Joseph." Mrs. Winkle consulted her
notes. "Ah yes, Joseph will be played by Michael Draper." Michael,
a boy with the cutest dimples and brown hair and eyes, ran up
onstage to the cheers and back slaps of the shepherds. EJ's heart
pounded a little harder. *Michael Draper as Joseph!*

*EJ stands, center stage, bathed in beautiful light shining from
above. This is her moment. She lovingly holds the tiny baby in her arms,
rocking him gently as peaceful music plays. At her feet are a goat and a*

sheep, watching the touching scene in silent awe.

"My beautiful baby boy, born in such a humble way, but will one day become my King and Savior." EJ delivers the line tenderly as a single tear slides down her cheek. She feels the audience's eyes on her and can already hear their adoring praise after the pageant:

"Oh, EJ, your portrayal of Mary made my Christmas complete."

"What a rare talent you are—next stop, Broadway!"

"You truly are a star, EJ."

EJ lays the tiny baby in the manger, tucks a blanket around him, and looks up as she feels Michael lay a gentle hand on her shoulder. He looks down at EJ and smiles, dimples and all. EJ's heart melts a little bit. EJ hears her music cue, takes a deep breath, and starts to sing in a clear voice.

"Silent night, holy night. All is calm, all is bright. . ."

"EJ, I admire your Christmas spirit, but I need you onstage for your costume fitting." Mrs. Winkle's voice snapped EJ out of her daydream. Had Mrs. Winkle already announced who was going to be playing Mary? EJ walked up onstage to the rack of costumes, hoping to see a Mary costume all ready for her.

"Can we do something about the drab colors?" CoraLee McCallister stepped out from behind the rack, tying a sash around Mary's brown robes.

No! No! No! EJ's brain screamed. First she wins the spelling bee and now this? It's not fair!

"Here's a little color for the Mary costume," Mrs. Anderson said as she handed CoraLee a blue head covering.

"I guess that will have to do," CoraLee snipped, making a face as she walked away. It took all of EJ's self-control not to grab the blue material, put it on her own head, and scream, "IF YOU DON'T WANT IT, I'LL TAKE IT!"

"EJ, I've got your costume right here." Mrs. Anderson pulled a hanger from the back of the rack and held it up to show EJ: a long, white robe that was trimmed around the neck in gold Christmas garland, a headband with an angel halo made out of the same garland, and giant angel wings that looked so awkward that EJ thought no angel wearing them could ever get two inches off the ground.

Tears stung in EJ's eyes as she stared at the costume. This wasn't what she wanted. Out of the corner of her eye, she saw CoraLee talking to Michael, both dressed as Mary and Joseph. Her starring role and time with Michael's cute dimples disappeared like a tray of Christmas cookies in front of a bunch of preschoolers.

"When I found out you were going to be our angel, I added a little something special to the costume." Mrs. Anderson pulled back a fold of the white robe material to reveal a sequined gold star on the chest of the costume. "When you were in my Sunday school class, I remember that you decorated all your crafts and Bible story papers with stars."

EJ smiled weakly and willed her eyes to dry up, touched by Mrs. Anderson's thoughtfulness. She'd been EJ's kindergarten Sunday school teacher. "Thank you, Mrs. Anderson," she said. "It's really nice."

A few minutes later, Mrs. Winkle assembled the fourth-grade cast, now in costume, for an inspection.

"Very nice, everyone. . . ." Mrs. Winkle adjusted a sash here and a collar there. "Sara, we'll need to let the hem of your robe out a bit, dear. . .no self-respecting wise guy in first-century Israel would ever allow so much of her shin to show."

EJ tugged at the tinsel garland that scratched her neck and thought even being a wise guy would be better than the angel.

"Here come our other players now." Mrs. Winkle waved in the groups of other kids, also in costume. "Let's get everyone

99

up onstage to set our spots for the finale, and we'll be done for tonight."

☆

"I just can't believe it," EJ lamented at the kitchen table at home after rehearsal. "I was *born* to play Mary. Maybe I'll just quit the pageant."

"EJ, you know that's not an option," Mom said, cutting chicken and putting it in a sizzling pan for stir-fry. "What's so bad about being the angel anyway?"

"You mean apart from the horrible costume and the fact that I'm onstage for a total of about thirty seconds?" EJ asked, laying placemats on the table. "By the end of it, nobody's even going to remember that I'm in the play."

Bert, drinking noisily from his water dish by the back door, padded over to EJ and looked up at her with comforting eyes. "You know what I'm talking about, don'tcha, Bert?" EJ picked him up and buried her face in his fur.

"I think you're underestimating the importance of the angel," Dad said, setting paper plates on each of the four placemats. "Without the angel to announce the birth of Jesus to the shepherds, how would anybody have known about it?"

"I dunno, I guess I never really thought about it." EJ shrugged and sat at the table, Bert on her lap.

"No TV, no news reporters, no cell phones to take a video and upload it to YouTube, no Twitter to make the big announcement," Dad said, placing silverware next to each plate. "The angel started a chain reaction of news sharing—from heaven to the shepherds who shared the news with everyone they saw, who then shared the news with others."

"So the angel was kind of breaking the biggest news story ever," EJ said. "I never thought about it like that."

"The biggest and one of the most important stories," Mom said, carrying the sizzling skillet of stir-fry to the table. "The baby would change the world forever."

EJ thought about that for a minute. That seemed pretty legit. Maybe the part of the angel wasn't *so* bad after all.

"Isaac, dinner!" Mom called as she filled the kids' glasses with milk and the parents' glasses with ice water.

"Mom, could we please do something about the garland on my costume? I think I'm starting to break out in hives," EJ said, scratching her neck where she could still feel the plastic garland cutting into her.

"I'll see what we can do," Mom said, smiling.

Isaac ran into the kitchen and hopped up onto his chair, licking his lips. "What's for dinner?"

"Your mom's delicious stir-fry," Dad said, helping Isaac tuck his napkin into the collar of his shirt.

"Yumm!" Isaac said, picking up a fork. "I would like that and a side of tin can, please."

"Tin can?" Mom asked, confused.

"Yeah!" Isaac said. "How else can I practice for my part as a goat in the nativity play?"

Everyone laughed.

Chapter 9

ANNE OF GREEN GABLES: PRIVATE EYE

Dear Diary,

Every year the church puts on a Fall Festival and invites all of Spooner. And since there's not much else to do around here, pretty much the whole town shows up for a brisk autumn evening in the churchyard for some apple bobbing, face painting, doughnuts and hot cider, carnival games, hayrides, costume judging, and the main event: a pie-eating contest. Other than Christmas and my birthday, it's probably my favorite day of the year.

Mom lets Isaac and me pick our own costumes for the festival. As long as they aren't evil or scary or too dumb, we can be whatever we want. When Isaac was three and just old enough to pick his costume, he chose to go as a light switch. A light switch.

What a weirdo, right?

Mom acted like it was the cutest thing she'd ever heard of in her life, so she rigged up a sweatshirt that had an oversized switch on his chest made out of an empty Kleenex box and a couple of wooden rulers. All night Isaac walked around the festival, one chubby toddler hand holding Dad's hand and the other flipping the switch up and down, proudly shouting two of his favorite words: "On! Off! On! Off! ON!" and then laughing like a crazy troll baby. Nobody, and I mean nobody, even noticed my delightfully witty costume Dad and I made by taping 124 rolls of Smarties to my jeans.

Smarty-pants—get it?

Apparently nobody else did, either.

This year, though. . .this year will be different. I am dressing up as a character who is so beloved by the entire world that I know I will simply be at the center of every conversation, the envy of everyone, the undisputed winner in every category of costume judging. Yes, dearest Diary: I am going as none other than Anne Shirley. Anne of Green Gables, the young orphan so imaginative and delightful that she dreams herself to have a better life than what she is actually living. The girl with two braids that are tragically and horribly the color of carrots but who imagines her hair to be a lovely auburn instead. Anne Shirley, my hero.

I can smell Mom's pumpkin pie baking in the oven, so it's time to go get in my costume, Diary. Later, alligator!

Anne with an "e"

Anne Shirley smoothes her gingham dress, straightens her straw hat, and makes sure that her two carrot-colored braids are lying just so on her shoulders. It isn't every day that's as special as the Fall Festival, and for an orphan who moved from foster home to foster home, finally having a community to belong to like this one is positively thrilling. She closes her eyes and imagines her red hair transforming to a beautiful shade of auburn, her freckles dissolving into a flawless complexion. She is the loveliest and luckiest girl in the world.

"First place for best fast-food costume goes to EJ Payne, dressed as Wendy!" a voice over the loudspeaker jolted EJ out of her daydream. "With her red braids and freckles, she looks exactly like the girl on the hamburger restaurant sign. Come on up here to get your prize, EJ!"

A crowd of costume-wearers applauded as EJ walked up to the podium, a little confused at what had just happened.

"I thought she was dressed as Pippi Longstocking," she heard someone say.

"Wendy? She looks more like Raggedy Ann to me," another person added.

The announcer pinned a blue ribbon on EJ's front and handed her the microphone. "Say something, if you want," he said, checking the list in front of him for the name of the next winner.

"Um, thanks," EJ said nervously into the mic. "But I'm not Wendy. I'm actually Anne Shirley." EJ looked out at the crowd and saw only blank stares. "You know, from Lucy Montgomery's beloved novel, *Anne of Green Gables*?"

The announcer snatched the mic back from EJ. "Never heard of it, but congratulations anyway." A few people clapped. "Now, on to the next category: best use of face paint in an animal costume. . ."

EJ walked away, not sure how she felt about her first-place ribbon. *I live in a town of entirely uncultured people*, she thought, *but a win* is *a win.* She decided to leave the ribbon pinned to her chest.

The Fall Festival was in full swing, with kids and adults alike dressed in costumes, milling around the churchyard, a chill in the autumn air. EJ saw a teenage girl from the youth group painting a butterfly on the cheek of a smiling toddler at the face-painting booth. Cory Liden, dressed as Batman, was at the next booth over, biting into a big, red apple that he had just bobbed out of a kiddie pool filled with water. A tractor pulling a flatbed wagon stacked with square bales of hay drove slow laps around the block, giving hayrides to kids hyped up on the candy they'd won at the game booths. And the food table was jam-packed with all the delicious flavors of the season: caramel apples, kettle corn, doughnuts, and hot cider. The only thing missing from the table was pumpkin pie, but those were all set up behind the church building for the pie-eating contest.

EJ stopped by the dunking booth where Dad was seated on the hot seat above the tank of water. There was a line of about a dozen people waiting for a chance to toss a softball at a small red-and-white target that, when hit, would drop the pastor into the water. This was Dad's favorite part of the festival every year.

"Hey, you throw like a girl!" Dad teased Sara Powers, who had just missed hitting the target by inches.

"A girl who is about to get you dunked, Pastor Payne!" Sara, who was a pitcher in girls' summer league softball, aimed and hurled the ball again, this time hitting the bull's-eye, dead center.

There was a half-second delay before the crowd heard a click and the small seat Dad sat on gave away. Dad yelped as he went into a freefall into the tank, sputtering and wiping his face with his hands as he broke the surface of the water. "Nice arm, Sara!" he said, laughing.

Dad reached up and pulled a chain at the back of the tank, resetting the seat. Then he crawled up to his perch, his hair, T-shirt, and trunks dripping wet. He looked down and saw EJ waving at him.

"Hey, EJ—did you win a prize?" Dad pointed at the blue ribbon on her chest.

"Oh, yeah." EJ chuckled to herself. "I won this for my *Wendy's* costume."

Dad looked puzzled for a second, but then his face brightened. "You know what? I see it," he said. "And Wendy, you make a *delicious* hamburger."

"Hey, look at this guy." Dad went back to razzing the people trying to dunk him, this time a muscular man named Ted. "I doubt he's strong enough to even throw the softb—"

Splash!

EJ found Mom working in the cotton-candy booth, hunched over the whirring air machine that fluffed the candy. She had the pointy end of a paper cone wedged in her hair, with a cloud of blue cotton candy on the end, announcing to everyone who walked by that this was the place to come get some cotton candy. Twirling another paper cone around the circle of the cotton-candy machine, Mom glanced up and saw EJ watching her. "Hi, hon!" Mom called over the noise of the machine. She handed the cone of cotton candy to the next kid in line, a transformer who looked mildly uncomfortable in his stiff Optimus Prime costume. "Having fun?"

"Yeah, I guess," EJ said, and then without thinking she said something that Mom *extremely disliked.* "I'm bored."

"Come on. . .*really*, EJ?" Mom stopped making cotton candy and put her hands on her hips. "Look around you! This is one of the least boring things we do all year! I don't say this very often, but you could learn a thing or two from Isaac tonight." Mom pointed an empty paper cone toward the hayride wagon. EJ looked and saw Isaac was sitting on one of the hay bales, proudly wearing a Smokey the Bear costume and lecturing a group of preschoolers about the dangers of hay fires. "You see this?" Isaac held up a handful of loose hay. "This stuff will burn faster than you can say, 'Only you can prevent forest fires,' and *that's* why you should never play with matches, kids." The four-year-olds and their parents seemed oddly spellbound by the words of the kid in a bear mask.

As the tractor rounded the corner, EJ heard Isaac/Smokey ask, "Hey, who wants to hear a joke? Knock-knock. . ."

EJ turned back to Mom, who held out a bag filled with pink cotton candy. "Here, now get sugared up and have some fun," she said, smiling.

🌟

EJ was sitting on a bench, nibbling cotton candy, when she felt a tap on her shoulder.

"EJ, can I sit with you?"

EJ looked up to see a kindergarten-sized Cinderella in front of her. Head to toe, the girl looked like the real thing complete with an updo, pearl earrings and necklace, beautiful blue ball gown, and glass slippers.

"These shoes hurt my feet."

EJ realized the Cinderella was Katy McCallister, CoraLee's little sister and the girl EJ "rescued" at family camp. "Oh yeah, sure." EJ scooted over to allow enough room for Katy's full skirt that looked like it had about eighteen layers of netting underneath to make it poof out.

"That costume is legit," EJ said. "Looks like the real Cinderella dress and shoes."

"They were my sister's," Katy said, shrugging. "I wanted to be a lion, but Mom said no, I need to be pretty like CoraLee was when she dressed up like a princess."

EJ thought it was dumb that Katy wasn't allowed to dress in the costume she wanted, but saying so might make Katy feel worse, so she decided to keep quiet.

"I like your Pippi Longstocking costume," Katy said.

"Anne of Green Gables," EJ corrected Katy, but seeing no spark of recognition in the little girl's eyes, she just mumbled, "Never mind." EJ stood up, ready to find something else to do. "See you later, Katy."

"Wait! EJ!" Katy took off her glass slippers and plopped them on the bench next to her. "I'm coming, too!"

EJ wanted to say, *"Get lost, kid,"* but she figured that when Katy saw how boring it was following her around, she'd probably get lost on her own. "Fine. Whatever," EJ said instead.

She started toward the backyard of the church (with Katy, now barefoot, trailing close behind), where there were two long tables set up on a platform for the pie-eating contest that would take place in a few minutes. A dozen pumpkin pies sat on the tables, ready for each contestant to take his or her place to chow down at the starting whistle.

As the girls turned the corner, EJ saw something strange: a boy dressed in black clothes, with a dark piece of cloth tied around his face like a train robber in an old Western, was hovering over the pies.

"Get down!" EJ whispered sharply to Katy, grabbing the girl's wrist and pulling her to her knees behind the back row of folding chairs that had been set up for the audience of the pie-eating contest.

"What's wrong?" Katy asked, wide-eyed. "Are we starting an adventure?"

EJ put her finger to her lips in a *shush* gesture.

"I know this is your first day on the private investigator beat,

Cindy, but you're going to have to learn how to follow my lead without making a lot of racket," Anne whispers to Cindy.

"See that person up there?" Anne jabs her thumb toward the masked mystery person. "He is up to no good. We need a better look."

Motioning Cindy to follow her, the private investigator and her young assistant crawl quickly on all fours one row, three rows, five rows closer to the stage where the shady business is going down.

Anne pulls out a small notepad and jots a few notes:

1. Suspect is male.

2. Suspect is dressed in black clothes.

3. Suspect seems to be doing something to the pies.

"May I have your attention?" a voice over the loudspeaker suddenly cut into EJ's daydream. "The pie-eating contest will start in five minutes. Please make your way to the backyard now, and we'll get started shortly."

And just like that, the masked guy jumped off the stage and sprinted away, clutching something in his hand. "Hey, you!" EJ yelled, standing up from her hiding spot in the folding chairs. "Yeah, stop!" Katy popped up and shouted. But he didn't turn around.

A crowd of spectators and contestants for the pie-eating contest streamed into the backyard and began to fill the seats—adults and kids alike, excited for the always-entertaining pie-eating contest.

EJ and Katy pushed through the crowd to try to see where the pie bandit went. Once they got clear of the sea of bodies, they couldn't see a dark-clothed person anywhere.

"Katy, you stay here and look for clues—anything that might tell us what he was doing," EJ said. "I'll go back and see if I can tell if there's anything wrong with the pies."

"Okay, you can count on me, EJ!" Katy said, crouching down to look closely at the ground where the pie bandit had run.

Dad, now dry and in a fresh set of clothes, was up onstage, acting as official judge for the pie-eating contest. When EJ had made her way back to the stage, he was already introducing each of the contestants.

"Back this year to defend his pie-eating title is Michael Draper—let's give him a big hand," Dad announced into the mic. Michael stood and waved to the crowd.

Trying to act as natural as possible, EJ creeped onstage and walked along the front of the tables, looking carefully at the pies as she passed each one.

Dad gave EJ a questioning look and held the mic behind his back before saying, "EJ, what are you doing? Your name's not on the list of contestants."

"Oh, no, Dad. . .I just wanted to. . .uh. . .make sure the pies are all pumpkin pies." EJ was making it up as she went along. "Just making sure no cherry pies accidentally got put up here."

"Pumpkin, pumpkin, pumpkin," EJ pretended to check each one off a mental checklist but didn't see anything out of the ordinary about any of the pies.

"Yep, looks good to go, Dad." She laughed nervously.

"Oookay." Dad raised an eyebrow at her. "Thank you?"

"No problem," EJ replied with a fake smile. "Happy to help."

Stumped, EJ stepped off the stage and took a seat in an empty chair in the front row. Dad went back to introducing the contestants, but at the end of the row, he came to an empty seat.

Dad read from the name tag in front of the empty space. "Cory Liden? Are you here, Cory?" The crowd murmured, looking around for the missing contestant.

"Here! I'm here!" Cory shouted from the back of the crowd, running up to the stage and taking his seat on the end. "Sorry I'm late." He slipped off his Batman mask and set it next to his pie, ready to go face-first into the delicious dessert.

EJ eyed Cory. Something was missing from his costume. She tried to remember what he looked like when she saw him earlier at the apple-bobbing booth.

"Now that we're all here, let's get started," Dad said into the mic, addressing the twelve contestants on the stage, mostly elementary-aged boys and a couple of dads. "This is a no-hands contest, so clasp your hands behind your back when I say to. The first person to finish their entire pie, including the crust, will be this year's winner. Everybody understand?"

The contestants nodded, ready to get started.

"All right, everyone," Dad called. "Hands behind your back. Ready. . .set. . .eat!" Dad blew a whistle to signal the beginning of the contest.

All twelve faces disappeared into their pics, and the crowd cheered them on. EJ watched carefully, looking for anything that might signal something was wrong with the pies. She was concentrating so hard that she didn't see Katy run up to her, out of breath.

"EJ *(inhale, exhale)*, look what I found in the big trash can over there!" Katy held up a black piece of material and a jar of pickles. "This jar of pickles was wrapped up in this black cape. Couldn't this be what the pie bandit used to cover his face?"

"Yeah! It could be. But pickles, what on earth?—" EJ took the pickle jar from Katy and looked at it a little closer. Inside were dill pickle spears, but no pickle juice!

"Ugh, my stomach hurts," Michael Draper groaned from the stage, making EJ look up. "This pie tastes really weird." Michael was sitting back in his chair, his face plastered with pumpkin custard and bits of crust. But more than half of his pie was still in the pan in front of him. Other contestants started groaning similar complaints and holding their stomachs until eleven of the twelve had stopped eating and were looking a little green. The only person left chowing down was Cory Liden, who was swallowing the last bit of crust at that very moment.

"Woooo! Yeah!" Cory stood and pumped his empty pie plate above his head. "I win! Take THAT, Michael!"

Michael and the other contestants looked at Cory in a daze, some of the crowd clapping for Cory, but most everyone was too distracted by how sick the rest of the contestants looked.

Suddenly a light bulb went off in EJ's head. She jumped up onto the stage, facing Cory. "Not so fast, Cory. . . . I have evidence that you rigged this contest so you could win."

"EJ, what are you talking about?" Dad asked, eyeing the eleven people onstage who still looked like their pie might come back up. "Why would Cory do that?"

"All I know is the how," EJ said. "Cory will have to tell us the why."

EJ launched into an explanation about seeing a boy dressed in all black, doing something to the contest pies.

"I didn't get a good look at his face because I was too far away," EJ explained, "but as you can see in Exhibit A, Cory is dressed in black from head to foot—as Batman. "

"There are lots of boys dressed in all-black costumes," Cory said defensively. "I can see three other Batmen out in the crowd right now."

"I'm not finished," EJ said.

Next EJ explained that the pie bandit ran from the scene, carrying an unidentified object, when the contest was announced over the loudspeaker.

"I didn't know what he had done to the pies until my assistant, Katy, brought me the evidence," EJ said, smiling at Katy. "But

ANNE OF GREEN GABLES: PRIVATE EYE

now I know that he laced the pies with pickle juice. Exhibit B!" She held up the pickle jar with the dramatic flair she'd seen in courtroom dramas on TV.

"Oooohhhh, yeah, that's *exactly* what this pie tastes like," Michael groaned. "It's not a good combination."

EJ stuck her finger in the uneaten part of Michael's pie, pulled it out, tasted it, and made a face. "Thoroughly disgusting. Nobody's going to be able to eat the whole thing."

"Except for me," Cory said, still cocky. "I ate the whole thing and won."

"Not so fast," EJ said, motioning Katy to come join her on the stage. "The pie bandit would've left his own pie pickle-juice free— guaranteeing his pie-eating contest win."

"You can't prove it!" Cory said. "Maybe someone else *wanted* me to win."

"When you took your spot for the contest, I couldn't figure out why your costume looked different—like it was missing something," EJ said. "But when Katy brought me the pickle jar she found in the trash can. . ."

"It was wrapped up in Cory's missing Batman cape. Exhibit C!" Katy finished, waving the cape over her head triumphantly. Cory reached a hand over his shoulder, grasping for his Batman cape that wasn't there.

"Ah yes, Cory, you didn't have much time, so you used what you had," EJ said, pressing her fingertips together. "Unfortunately, what you had linked you to the crime."

Cory went pale.

"Okay, okay. . . I think the word *crime* is a little melodramatic, EJ," Dad said. Then he put a hand on Cory's shoulder and said quietly, "Cory, is what EJ said true? Did you put pickle juice on the pies?"

"Yeah, I did, Pastor Payne." Cory looked defeated. "I just wanted to beat Michael."

"Beat Michael? Why?" Dad asked.

"I dunno. He won last year, and he's been bragging about getting the role of Joseph in the Christmas play," Cory said, crossing his arms. "I guess I was just tired of always being second place to him."

"I'll need to speak to your mom about this, Cory. Thankfully, pickle juice pumpkin pies won't do much more damage than a stomachache." Dad put the mic back up to his mouth. "Moms and dads, if you have a son up here, would you come and get him? A dose of Pepto-Bismol might be just what the doctor ordered."

The crowd started to thin as families headed home.

"Bye, EJ—thanks for including me!" Katy called as she left with her mom.

"Katy, where are your shoes? And is that a grass stain I see on your Cinderella dress?" she heard Mrs. McCallister ask, exasperated.

EJ watched Cory sit and put his pumpkin-pie plastered head in his hands. She knew what it was like to come in second place—maybe Cory felt about Michael the same way EJ felt about CoraLee.

"For the record, I think you would make a good Joseph," EJ said quietly.

"For the record, I think you would make a good Mary," Cory said, looking up at her. "Actually, what I *really* wanted was for us to play Mary and Joseph together." He cocked his head and gave her a small smile. "Next year?"

"Sounds like a plan." EJ smiled and blushed a little.

Maybe dimples were overrated.

Chapter 10

FIRST SNOW

Dear Diary,

Snow! Snow, snow, snow, snow! It's snowing! Not just a light dusting or a few sparkly flakes that remind you of one of the seventy-three snow globes that Mrs. Winkle uses to decorate her living room in August when it's eighty-five degrees outside ("They help me think cool thoughts, dear," she told me once), but honest-to-goodness Wisconsin snow. Perfect for snowballs, snowmen, snow forts, snow angels, and my very favorite: sledding!

When Isaac woke up this morning and saw the world blanketed in white, the crazy kid showed up at the breakfast table in his snowsuit, complete with toboggan hat, scarf, and mittens attached by a string that goes through his sleeves. (Babies like him wear mittens like that so they don't lose them.) I graduated to stringless gloves when I was four, but Isaac has never been as advanced as I am. Dad laughed and said he liked Isaac's enthusiasm, but we need to wait until the snow lets up a bit before we go outside and explore, which is fine with me. I'm content just watching from my bedroom window. Right now big, fluffy flakes are coming down as if the angels ripped open a million pillows in heaven's biggest-ever pillow fight.

I'm going to go help Dad sort out our snow toys in the garage so I can get first dibs on the best sled: the red saucer with the super-slick bottom and good hand grips. I see a new world record in my future!

"I'm cold," EJ whined as she dragged her kid-size snow shovel behind her.

"It's because you're walking too slowly, EJ." Dad looked over his shoulder and smiled.

It wasn't that EJ didn't want to be outside—it was that she didn't want to be outside to *work*. Dad promised they would get to play, but first they were walking to Mr. Johnson's house to shovel snow from his sidewalk and driveway. "To be a blessing," Dad said. EJ said they could be a blessing by staying away from a man who didn't want anybody to touch his property. Or, better yet, by building a snow fort in the park and letting Mr. Johnson watch them have fun from his living room and remember the "good old days." Dad said that wasn't the kind of blessing he was talking about.

"Come on, EJ. Gotta keep the blood flowing! I'll race you guys to Mr. Johnson's house. Ready?"

"But. . ." EJ's next complaint was going to be that there's no way she could run in a snowsuit.

"Set!" shouted Isaac, bundled from head to toe. It was a miracle he could make a sound from behind the scarf wound around and around his head.

"GO!" Dad took off like a flash with the handle of his shovel propped on his shoulder, his snow boots kicking up fresh snow behind him. Isaac followed close behind, dragging a tiny shovel.

Bert, also bundled in a hat and a coat, looked up at EJ inquisitively. *That looks like fun! Why aren't we running?* he seemed to be saying.

"Oh, all right." EJ grinned down at Bert. "Let's go!"

A few minutes later, Dad, Isaac, EJ, and Bert all stood at the edge of Mr. Johnson's driveway as Dad surveyed their work area.

EJ noticed a new hand-lettered sign in the front window:

IF YOU'RE SELLING IT, I DON'T NEED IT.
I'M DIABETIC; I WON'T BUY YOUR GIRL SCOUT COOKIES
OR SPORTS LEAGUE CANDY BARS.
I'M ALREADY PAYING TAXES;
I WON'T SPONSOR YOUR SCHOOL FUND-RAISER.

"Uh, Dad, are you sure this is a good idea?" EJ asked, pointing to the sign.

"Yeah, Dad—maybe he really just wants to be left alone," Isaac added, looking nervous.

"We're not going to bother him, guys," Dad said. He unzipped his coat pocket, took out a small envelope, and slipped it into Mr. Johnson's mailbox. "If we're quiet enough, he won't even know we're here. Now, let's figure out our territories."

"Figuring out their territories" was the first step of Dad's way of making snow shoveling into a game. Using the handle of his shovel, Dad etched out lines in the snow that showed which part each one of them was responsible for. Whoever cleared their section fastest was the winner. Today the winner would get an extra fifteen snowballs to start out in the snow war they were planning for later—a prize that all three desperately wanted to win.

Dad's territory was by far the biggest, taking up most of the driveway and the short path up to Mr. Johnson's porch ("If he comes out, I want him to sic Gruff on me instead of you guys," Dad said with a grin. "I've got so many layers on that it'll take him a good ten minutes to scratch through them, and that'll give you guys time to get away."); EJ's territory was smaller, but took up some of the end of the driveway; Isaac's territory was the smallest (but EJ knew it was fair because his shovel was so small)—the sidewalk connecting Mr. Johnson's driveway to his mailbox. Bert didn't have a territory; he was just there for support.

"Ready, you two?" Dad whispered. "Go!"

Three shovels dug in, and the snow started flying.

Dad threw the snow over his shoulder, and Bert barked excitedly, hopping through the white stuff as it cascaded down, biting at it playfully.

"*Shh*, Bert!" EJ whispered, glancing nervously at the house. "That grouchy cat will hear you!"

Too late. She saw the cat's head poke through the blinds that covered the front window, and even though she couldn't hear it, the look on the cat's face made it obvious that he was hissing. . . loudly.

"Uh-oh. Gruff alert!" EJ said, pointing. "We'd better hurry."

"Faster, guys!" Dad said, shifting his shovel action into high gear. "Mr. Johnson doesn't move too quick these days, so it'll take him a little while to get to the window. By the way, I think I'm winning!"

"No, I'm winning!" Isaac's little shovel was working a mile a minute.

"Done! I'm done!" EJ announced gleefully before realizing she was shouting, possibly blowing their cover. Bert jumped happily at EJ, and she dropped her shovel to catch him in her arms. His warm tongue licked her cheek, and she laughed.

"Nice job, EJ!" Dad said shoveling the last bit of snow off his territory. Then he finished up Isaac's area with one swift swipe of his full-size shovel. "I think that was the fastest job we've ever done."

"Fearing for my life helps me work faster," EJ said, still eyeballing the front window of the house.

Dad picked up EJ's shovel and glanced over his shoulder at the window where Gruff still looked through the blinds, now pawing at the glass like he wanted to attack. In a split second, the blinds shot up, revealing Mr. Johnson standing at the window with an angry look on his face. Actually, EJ wasn't sure if it was an angry look or not—but it was the same look he always had on his face.

Dad waved and smiled at Mr. Johnson from the end of the driveway. EJ (still holding Bert in her arms) and Isaac hid behind him. "Hello, Mr. Johnson—hope you're doing well!" Dad called. "Isn't the snow beautiful?"

And just like that, the blinds snapped back down into place. Apparently Mr. Johnson liked small talk about as much as he liked trespassers.

"Let's head home, guys," Dad said, looking thoughtfully at Mr. Johnson's house. "Mom will have lunch ready for us, and then we've got that epic snow war to fight."

⭐

After lunch, the Paynes spent the rest of the afternoon outside, except for a thirty-minute break that Mom insisted they take— but it included hot cocoa and chocolate-chip cookies, so it wasn't so bad.

They split into two teams for the backyard snow war: Mom and EJ on one side, and Dad and Isaac on the other. EJ and Mom chose the picnic table (propped on its side to act as a shield) to be their home base, and Dad and Isaac chose their swing set clubhouse as their home base. The boys' choice of home base proved to be their undoing, though—because they had to go up and down the ladder to reload snowballs.

"We surrender! We surrender!" Dad called from the much-too-small-for-an-adult clubhouse as Mom and EJ pelted the boys with snowball after snowball through the clubhouse entrance.

Mom and EJ dropped their snowballs and helped Dad crawl out of the cramped clubhouse. Isaac hopped down easily after him.

"Boy, we got whipped," Dad said to Isaac as he brushed snow away from his coat and hat. "These Payne women are quite the snow warriors."

"You fellas can redeem yourself on the sledding slopes," Mom said, her eyes twinkling. "Double or nothing?"

"You're on!" Dad said.

The sledding contest at Spooner Park ended in a tie: Mom and EJ winning for speed and Dad and EJ winning for distance. Even Bert got in on the action by going down the hill with EJ on a saucer, yipping and scratching the whole way down. Apparently Bert liked watching more than he liked sledding.

Back home, each Payne made a snowman in his or her own likeness in the front yard. ("SnowPaynes" Dad called them.) Mom gave her SnowPayne a bun on top of her head and put so many little sticks in the bun that Isaac said it looked like she had a porcupine on her head. Dad used an old pair of his glasses and propped them on the face of his SnowPayne. "So the neighbors know which one is me," he said.

The Isaac SnowPayne had the T-Rex mask (the one Bruce wore in the Payne-fully Spectacular Circus) for a head, sticks for arms, and an extra pair of Isaac's stringed mittens slipped on the end of the arms, the string hooked through the T-Rex's teeth.

EJ was particularly proud of her SnowPayne. She had raided the craft closet and found little plastic gems of all colors that she poked into the surface of the snow to create the details on her snow girl. Green sparkly eyes and ruby-red lips and a multicolored star over her heart. As a final touch, EJ grabbed an old pair of Converse All Stars from the garage and put them at the bottom of SnowPayne EJ.

"My, we are quite the family!" Mom said. "You three, stand next to your SnowPaynes, and I'll take a picture."

Dad, EJ, and Isaac smiled while Mom took a picture with her phone. "Wait a minute," Mom said, looking down at the screen. "Which one is the real Isaac? They look so much alike that I can't tell the difference!"

✪

"Dad, why did you want to shovel Mr. Johnson's driveway, anyway?" EJ asked as they unloaded sleds from the minivan before heading inside to warm up. "He didn't want us there. He didn't even say 'thank you.' "

Dad considered her question for a moment.

"I wanted us to help out Mr. Johnson because he's the kind of person we're called to show kindness to," Dad said. "I don't know why he is grouchy and mean, but it doesn't really matter what the reason is. Because one way we live out our faith is by loving the people who are mean to us."

"I guess," EJ said, unconvinced. "But what if someone is *always* mean to you?"

"Doesn't matter." Dad shook his head. "If I'm kind only to the people who will do something good for me in return, who will treat me kind back, then that's not fully living the way Jesus wants me to."

That sounded hard to EJ. Maybe even impossible.

"No, Bert! Stop!" Isaac shouted angrily. "That's *my* mitten!"

EJ and Dad turned around just in time to hear a *riiip* of cloth and see Bert run outside of Isaac's short reach, Isaac's right mitten in his mouth.

Bert's eyes danced as he ran and hopped in the snow, inches away from Dad's fingertips. "Get back here, you mutt!" Dad called good-naturedly. EJ laughed, knowing "keep-away" was one of Bert's favorite games.

"My hand is cooooold!" Isaac howled, holding up his naked right hand. "And Bert broke my mitten string!"

"Here, ya baby." EJ slipped her glove onto her brother's small hand and shoved her own hand in her coat pocket to keep warm. "Looks like Bert thought it was about time for you to graduate to big-kid gloves without a string."

After a few more seconds of the chase, Dad caught Bert and rescued the mitten.

"Here you go, buddy." Dad handed the mitten to Isaac. "One big-kid glove for you."

Chapter 11

THE PILOT'S PREDICAMENT

Dear Diary,

It's Saturday morning, and Mom has a list of chores we are supposed to get done today. In an effort to delay starting the laundry, I have already taken as long as humanly possible to finish my cereal and orange juice, change out of my pj's, and brush my teeth. (I counted 564 circles with the toothbrush before Mom hollered that she was going to put me on dusting duty instead of laundry if I didn't hurry up already. Fast fact: I despise dusting.) But then, in a last-ditch effort, I asked Mom if I could please take ten minutes to write a highly important diary entry. And abracadabra, here I am!

I have another career to add to my list, Diary: presidential helicopter pilot. I read an article on Wikipedia about the Marine helicopters that transport the President of the United States on many of his important trips.

Whenever the president is riding in one of these helicopters, it's given the call sign of

"Marine One." The article said the pilots are part of the "HMX-1 Nighthawks" squadron. Have you ever heard of a cooler name? As soon as I read that, I was sold. Another super spy-like part of transporting the president around is that Marine One never flies alone—they always fly in a group of as many as five identical helicopters, one carrying the president and the others as decoys.

As preparation for becoming a Marine helicopter pilot, I'll work on my hand/eye coordination by challenging Dad to more games of air hockey in the church's youth room. And then after Dad beats me, I'll play against Isaac.

I can always beat him.

Marine One, over and out,

EJ

EJ dragged an overflowing laundry basket through the doorway into the laundry room.

She stood staring at the mountain of dirty clothes, hands on hips, letting her dislike of laundry duty bubble up inside.

"Seriously, why do we have to own so many clothes?" EJ shouted at no one in particular. "I'd be perfectly happy with one pair of jeans and a couple of shirts!" She reached down, pinched a tiny corner of one of Isaac's socks, and tossed it away like it was diseased.

"Good job, you're sorting the laundry like I showed you." Mom poked her head in the doorway of the laundry room, the handle of a feather duster stuck in her bun. The effect of the feathers sticking straight out of her head reminded EJ of a peacock. "Here, I have some more for you." She set down a second full laundry basket.

"You're *killing* me, Mom," EJ whined. Mom chose to ignore the comment.

"Oh, and there are two reasons why we have to own so many clothes," Mom said, grabbing the handle of the vacuum cleaner that stood next to the dryer. "Number one, we have to wear clothes because Eve really ruined the whole naked thing when she ate the forbidden fruit."

"I didn't say I wanted to be *naked*," EJ corrected her. "I said I'd just want jeans and a couple of shirts."

"And number two," Mom continued, "if you only had jeans and a couple of shirts, you'd be in here doing the laundry a *lot* more often than once a week, just so you'd have clean clothes to wear. Still think your idea is a good one?" Mom smiled sweetly at EJ.

"No," EJ muttered. "I take it back."

"All right then, keep up the good work," Mom said, wheeling

the vacuum out the door. "Isaac and I are off to vacuum, dust, and change the linens on the beds."

EJ sighed and focused her attention back to the piles of laundry in front of her. Before she started sorting again, she heard Bert's doggie paws on the tile floor as he came to see what was going on. EJ grinned at her canine friend.

"Well, if I have to be doing something as boring as the laundry, at least I can do it with you," EJ said, patting Bert on the head. "Wanna give me a hand with this?"

Bert jumped onto one of the piles and surveyed the room from his mountain peak. EJ wished she had her dog's ability to find fun in something as utterly terrible as dirty clothes.

"Let's see. . . " EJ thought out loud, which was okay since Bert was the only one in the room. "What could we imagine to make laundry a little more interesting?"

EJ adjusts the pack on her back and shields her eyes against the midday sun before looking to see where Bert has gone. She whistles, and her loyal pup comes to her side.

"See that, Bert?" EJ points to the rocky bluffs above them. "We will conquer this mountain and claim it as ours, or my name isn't Emma Jean 'the Mountaineer' Payne!"

Bert barks his agreement, and the two head up the mountain pass, picking up samples of nature along the way.

EJ used a white undershirt in her hand to pick up a pair of white underwear and a few tube socks. She tossed the wad of white onto the whites pile and continued on.

"What is it, boy? What did you find?" EJ kneels down next to Bert to see what he's chewing on.

Bert obediently drops what's in his mouth. . . .

It was EJ's favorite Ohio State T-shirt, now complete with Bert bite holes in it.

"Aww, Bert!" EJ shook the now-ruined shirt at the dog. "This is *not* food! Bad dog!"

Bert whined and put his paw over his face, giving EJ his famous *I'm sorry* look. She couldn't stay too mad at him for long.

"Listen, you can't be in here if you're just going to chew on stuff," EJ said as she grabbed a dog toy from his kennel in the corner of the room. "I mean, I guess if you chewed up all the clothes, I wouldn't have to wash them. . . ." She thought about that for a second. "But I'd rather wash all the clothes in the world than be in *that* much trouble with Mom."

She tossed the chew toy to Bert and started sorting again.

EJ looks up and sees a covered wagon, surrounded by a sea of prairie grass rippling gently in the wind. The breeze catches the front edge of her bonnet, whisking it off her head, straight for the wagon. EJ runs after it, realizing she's dressed in a gingham prairie dress as well.

She leans down to get the rogue bonnet that's caught in the spokes of the wagon wheel. Just then a girl who looks to be a couple of years younger than EJ comes around the corner of the wagon, carrying a metal tub filled with soapy water.

"Are you done sorting the clothes, EJ?" asks the girl with long, dark braids and freckles on her nose. "Ma wants us to get started right away so we can be done before the sun goes down."

"But you—you're Laura Ingalls Wilder!" EJ points at the girl, eyes wide. "Little House on the Prairie! Half-pint! You're one of my favorite authors!"

"Yes, I'm Laura Ingalls. Pa calls me 'Half-pint,' " Laura says, setting the tub of water on the ground between them. "Maybe someday I'll get around to writing a book, but right now we've got laundry to do. Shall we get started?"

"We shall!" EJ says, tying her bonnet strings loosely around her neck. She begins working alongside Laura with a renewed interest in

laundry. EJ is amazed at how quickly and efficiently Laura sorts the laundry into neat piles.

"There. Now onto the soaking and scrubbing," Laura says matter-of-factly, dipping a shirt into the tub of water.

"Soaking and scrubbing?" EJ wrinkles her nose. "I figured we'd just use the washer and dryer in the laundry room."

"I don't know those words you're saying—wash-er and dry-er?" Laura asks, scrubbing the shirt on the side of the tub. The whole thing looks like way too much work to EJ. "Come on, EJ, we have to get this done or Ma will be cross."

"Uh, no thanks," EJ says. "I like reading about your life in the nineteenth century, Half-pint, but I think I like living in the twenty-first century when it comes to chores."

"Suit yourself, EJ," Laura says, working so hard at scrubbing the shirt that she's already broken out into a sweat.

EJ was relieved to see that she had managed to get the laundry all sorted into three piles (whites, lights, and darks) during her *Little House on the Prairie* daydream. Now it was time to get the wash started.

She set the water temperature on the washer to warm, the load level to large, and shoved the pile of white clothes through the circular door before shutting it tight. Then she opened a little pull-out drawer and carefully poured liquid detergent just to the fill line (like Mom had shown her), and pushed in the drawer till she heard a click.

"All systems are ready for launch," EJ said, trying to make the process a little more exciting than it really was. "Three. . .two. . . one. . .wash!" She pushed the START button to begin the washing cycle.

She flopped down on the floor and grabbed Bert's toy, still in his mouth. A few minutes of tug-of-war and fetch with the pooch and the washing machine had only gone through the first stage of its cycle.

EJ sighed and drummed her fingers on the floor. "Bert, I can't take much more of this," she said, pulling Bert onto her lap and stroking his soft fur. "Can a person die of boredom? Because I think I'm getting close."

The washing machine made a small lurch, stopping before it started its first spin cycle. EJ watched and listened to the drum spin around and around.

"That sound seems so familiar," EJ said, setting Bert down and crawling toward the washing machine on all fours, listening closely.

"Marine One, do you copy?" the voice crackles in EJ's headphones. "You are to report at the White House lawn at oh-eight-hundred-hours."

EJ looks around to see that she's in a helicopter cockpit, Bert in a Marine jumpsuit in the copilot seat next to her. She grips the helicopter's control in front of her—called a cyclic—and raises the chopper off the ground.

"Control, this is Marine One," EJ reports into the microphone attached to her communication headset. "I copy. Where is the president headed today?"

"To Buckingham Palace for tea with the Queen of England," comes the response from control. "Try to make sure he doesn't wrinkle his suit on the way over."

The pilot chuckles to herself. "I'll see what I can do, control," she says. "Over and out."

EJ checks the time on the helicopter control panel. She needs to refuel before she takes the president all the way across the Atlantic Ocean, and she barely has enough time to stay on schedule.

Pulling back on the cyclic, EJ steers Marine One toward the White House. Above her she sees blue sky and fluffy, white clouds, and below her she sees the impressive buildings and monuments of the nation's capital: the Capitol building, the Smithsonian museums, the Washington Monument, the Reflecting Pool, and in the distance, the Lincoln Memorial.

A few minutes later, Marine One touches down on the south lawn of the White House and the helicopter engine grinds to a halt. EJ unbuckles her seat belt and jumps out for a quick refueling.

EJ popped open the washing-machine door and transferred the clean clothes to the dryer. She added one dryer sheet to the load (sniffing it first—she loved the smell of fabric softener), shut the door, set the timer, and pushed START. Even while she was back in reality, she felt the pressure of the president's schedule that was waiting for her back in her daydream.

"Darks—check!" She stuffed the entire pile of dark clothes in the washer and pushed the door shut. "Extra large load—check!" She pushed the button and heard the water start to fill the machine. "Soap—check!" She opened the detergent drawer, quickly dumped some soap in the reservoir, and slammed it shut.

"Let's go, Bert. . . . The president can't be late for tea!" EJ picked Bert up, set him on top of the washing machine, and climbed up, too.

"Control, this is Marine One," EJ speaks into her headset. "Ready and in place for the president to board."

"Copy that, Marine One," control responds. "The president is exiting the White House now."

EJ starts the engine and begins her preflight checks: fuel levels are good, wind speed is within normal limits. . . .

"Good morning, EJ! How are you today, Bert?" The president steps into the helicopter, pats Bert on the head, and takes his seat in the back, buckling in. "Are we all set?"

"Morning, sir." EJ gives a little salute. "Just waiting for the go-ahead from control. I think we're still waiting for arrival of the decoy choppers."

"Ah, yes. . .the fake ones," the president says. "We should put dummies dressed as me in those other helicopters when we're flying, but some of my political rivals might say they can't tell the difference between the dummies and me!" He laughs good-naturedly, and EJ smiles.

"Good one, sir. Looks like the decoy choppers are arriving now," she says. "We'll be in the air in just a moment."

The president unfolds today's newspaper and disappears behind it.

"Marine One, you are clear for takeoff," control says.

"Copy that, control," EJ says, slipping on her aviator sunglasses.

She pulls back on the cyclic, and the helicopter rises above the tree line, joining the four decoy choppers. She steers the helicopter east, in formation just like they practice in drills. In a few short minutes, they are over the open waters of the Atlantic Ocean. The reflection of the sun sparkles on the surface of the calm sea. EJ breathes in the salty ocean air and thinks about how lucky she is to have a job like this.

Suddenly, the helicopter jolts violently, kind of like the engine has the hiccups. Bert barks at the instrument panel.

"Everything okay up there?" The president peeks over the top of his newspaper.

"Nothing to worry about, sir." EJ struggles with the cyclic to keep the helicopter flying straight and smooth. She frantically scans the instrument panel, looking for a reading on what might be happening.

Try as she might, EJ continues to lose altitude. With each hiccup of the engine, the helicopter comes closer to the water below.

"Mr. President, I've got good news and bad news," EJ says, struggling to keep the helicopter above water.

"Give me the good news first," the president says, calmly slipping on a life jacket and snapping the buckles.

"The good news is that I don't think we need to worry about your suit being wrinkled for tea with the queen," EJ says. "But the bad news is that your suit will most definitely be wet! Prepare for impact, sir!"

EJ grabs Bert and secures a life jacket around both of them, Bert's head sticking out just below EJ's chin and his hind legs dangling in midair from the bottom. EJ grasps the cyclic and makes one final mighty maneuver that lets the helicopter slide into the water instead of slamming into it.

Water immediately begins to fill the cockpit. Water. . .and soapsuds?

"Sir, don't panic," EJ calls to the president, who is still calmly reading his newspaper. "The Marines in the decoy choppers will have us out in a moment."

Her headset crackles a bit of static, but all EJ hears is, "Stop!"

"Say again, control?" EJ shouts. "You're breaking up."

"Code water! Code soapsuds! Code stop the washer!"

EJ snapped out of her daydream to see Dad standing in the doorway, shouting to be heard over the noise of the overfilled washing machine that was belching water and soapsuds onto the tile floor. From her seat on top of the washing machine, she reached down and pushed a button to stop the cycle.

"Oh no." EJ moaned, taking in the sight: too many clothes stuffed into the washing machine plus too much detergent equaled the mess she saw in front of her. Bert yipped happily in the suds, but he was the only one in the room who was excited.

EJ heard the vacuum cleaner turn off. "Everything okay, David?" Mom called from upstairs. "I heard shouting. . . ."

"No problem!" Dad called back. "EJ and I are going to give the laundry-room floor a deep clean—didn't you say you wanted to do that soon?"

"Oh yeah—that sounds great. Thanks!" The vacuum cleaner revved up again.

"Dad, I'm sorry," she said, looking grateful at the same time. "I didn't mean—I just—I did it again."

"Come on down," Dad said. "I'll help you clean this up."

EJ crawled down, careful not to slip in the soapy water on the floor while Dad pulled enough of the wet clothes out of the washing machine so that it wouldn't overflow again.

"That must've been some daydream," he said, raising an eyebrow at EJ while restarting the wash.

"Oh, you know, nothing special." EJ grabbed a stack of beach towels out of the linen closet and started mopping up the soapy water on the floor. "Just flying the president to Buckingham Palace for tea with the queen." She glanced at Dad out of the corner of her eye to see what his reaction would be.

"Cuppa tea? And crumpets? How delightful!" Dad said in his best English accent before turning serious. "But next time, EJ, the president can wait an extra minute or two so you can take the time you need to do the laundry the way Mom taught you. Got it?"

"Got it, Dad. . . . I promise," EJ said, using a second towel to wipe up more water. She wondered if she'd ever grow out of daydreaming for fun. Apparently the rest of the world thought she was already too old to have such a vivid imagination anyway.

"Arrrgh, ye landlubber. . . Ye be swabbing the poopdeck a little too slowly for me liking," Dad said. He dropped to his knees next to EJ and started drying the floor, too. "We got ter make this ship shine like new or we'll face the wrath of the most dreaded pirate in these waters—Mombeard!"

EJ laughed. Or maybe she'd never grow out of it. That was fine with her.

Chapter 12

GIVING THANKS

November 27

Dear Diary,

Tomorrow is Thanksgiving, so the house is filled with all kinds of amazing smells because Mom and Dad have been preparing food for tomorrow's feast. Dad's world-famous apple pie is cooling on the countertop, and Mom's orange-cranberry Jell-O salad just went in the fridge. Now she's starting a batch of her homemade dinner rolls. Just thinking about a roll fresh out of the oven, split open and slathered with melting butter makes my mouth water. (I'd sneak you one, Diary, but since you have no mouth or taste buds, you'll just have to take my word on how fantastic they are.)

The very best thing about Thanksgiving this year is that Mom's younger sister, Cara Jean, is coming. Aunt CJ is honestly the very best, most amazing adult I know. I'm named after her (we share the same middle name), and she grew up in Ohio in an even smaller town than Spooner (shocking, I know. . .), but after she graduated from high school, she went to college in Texas, got her journalism degree, and got a reporter job at the Chicago Tribune. I cannot wait to hear her stories about important assignments, investigative reporting, and glamorous interviews she gets to do for her job.

With all this writing I've been doing in you, Diary, journalism might be something for me to consider, too.

By EJ Payne, star reporter

"Hey, do you guys want to hear a joke?" Isaac poked his head into the video chat frame in front of EJ so his not-quite-so-bald spot stared her right in the face.

"Wait your turn, Space Invader." EJ pushed him out of the way. "I'm talking with Nana and Pops now!"

EJ was sitting on the couch in the living room, the family laptop on the coffee table in front of her. On the screen, she could see Mom's parents, Nana and Pops, on a video chat from their house in Ohio.

"Hey, be nice, EJ. Isaac misses his grandparents, too," Dad said, poking his head in from the kitchen. "And Isaac, be patient. You'll get your turn in a minute or two."

"And yes, Isaac, we do want to hear that joke in a few minutes!" Nana called to him from the speaker. "Now, EJ, you were telling us about your spelling bee?"

"Well, I came in second place, and I was really bummed," EJ said, watching the expressions on her grandparents' faces on the screen. "But *then* I found out that the top three spellers get to advance to the next level! I've been studying really hard."

"And she's absolutely going to kill the next one." Aunt CJ slid onto the couch right next to EJ and waved at the webcam to her mom and dad. "Hi, Mom—Hi, Dad! What's new in Ohio?"

EJ beamed at her aunt, only half hearing the conversation as CJ, Nana, and Pops chatted about what was new in Ohio. CJ had the prettiest blue eyes and blond curls that fell just past her chin. When EJ imagined her aunt on the job in the newsroom, she could see her in a crisp button-up shirt, dress pants, high heels, and perfect makeup—a reporter's notebook in one hand and a pen in the other, feverishly taking notes for the big story. Today for Thanksgiving, CJ was wearing a dark blue cotton dress with a wide brown belt, brown leggings, and brown ballet flats. She had a few curls pinned back from her face with a jeweled butterfly barrette.

"EJ. Hey, EJ, are you still with us?" Pops was saying on the computer screen. "I asked you how rehearsals are going for the Christmas pageant."

"Oh, yeah—sorry. They're fine," EJ said unenthusiastically. "Dad said he'll get a video of the play and upload it so you can see it, if you really want to."

"Of course we want to see you—and Isaac, too!" Nana said. "We're looking forward to it. And we really can't wait to visit you guys again. Hopefully in the spring."

"*After* Wisconsin is done getting its thirteen feet of snow for the year," Pops added, grinning.

"Is it my turn now?" Isaac hopped on one foot impatiently.

"Isaac is going to take his turn now," EJ said to her grandparents, scooting off the couch to make room for her brother. Then she added, "Get ready for the lamest joke you've ever heard in your life!"

"Aw, come on, EJ, it can't be *that* bad," Aunt CJ said, snuggling up with Isaac in front of the laptop.

"Oh, trust me—it's bad," Isaac said, nodding seriously. Then he turned to face the webcam and started the joke in his best stand-up comic voice: "Knock-knock!"

"Who's there?" EJ heard her grandparents ask in unison as she walked toward the kitchen.

"Noah." Isaac's voice faded as EJ stepped into the kitchen. EJ decided she really needed to help Isaac find another joke or two to add to his routine.

"EJ, come help set the table," Mom said, motioning her over to the dinner table—extra large with the leaf in place so it was big enough for everyone who was coming for the Thanksgiving meal. The four Paynes plus Aunt CJ and Mrs. Winkle made six.

EJ counted seven plates in the stack. "Mom, I think you have one too many plates out," she said. "There are only six of us."

"Seven," Dad said, adding ice to the glasses at the refrigerator. "I just found out yesterday that our seventh guest is a yes."

"Who—?" EJ's question got cut off when Mrs. Winkle came through the back door, her arms loaded with a casserole dish and a large tote bag that EJ figured must be holding an original Mrs. Winkle table centerpiece for the occasion.

"Happy Thanksgiving, Paynes!" she said, making a grand entrance like always.

Mom took the casserole dish from her and smiled. "So glad to have you, Wilma! EJ, would you take Mrs. Winkle's coat and hang it in the front closet?"

"Mrs. Winkle, may I take your coat?" EJ asked, stepping up to her neighbor, arms outstretched.

"Why, yes—thank you, dear." EJ helped Mrs. Winkle shrug out of her coat—a dark pink wool coat with green squares on it. But what was underneath the coat was even more fabulously shocking. When Mrs. Winkle realized EJ was staring, openmouthed, at her sweater, she did a turn to let her get a better look.

"What do you think, EJ?" she asked. "I used a boring old sweater I already had and Thanksgiving-ified it this morning."

Mrs. Winkle had taken a brown sweater and added an array of colored feathers to the back, with the tops of the feathers sticking up above her shoulders. The front of the sweater had a smiling turkey face on it, so the effect from the front was like Mrs. Winkle's entire torso was a cartoonish turkey.

"It's amazing!" EJ said, still awestruck.

"There are a lot of things I like about you, Mrs. Winkle," Dad said, putting an arm around her shoulders. "But one thing I really love is your commitment to always go big."

"What is it you kids say, David?" Mrs. Winkle asked, eyes sparkling. "Go big or go home!"

"That's right," said Dad, laughing.

EJ had just closed the closet door after hanging up Mrs. Winkle's coat when the doorbell rang.

Must be the mystery seventh guest, she thought to herself. She got a little thrill from the surprise of who it might be as she got up on tiptoe to look through the peephole. But who was standing there was probably the last person on earth she would've expected.

"Mr. Johnson?" she whispered. It couldn't be! She'd never even seen him outside his house, except for when he was working on his yard or chasing kids off his property, shaking his fist at them. She shook her head to get whatever cobwebs were there and looked again.

Still Mr. Johnson.

"I heard the doorbell—let's invite our guest in, EJ," said Dad. EJ turned toward Dad, wide-eyed and speechless.

"It's okay," Dad whispered and winked. "I invited him. Remember the envelope I put in his mailbox when we shoveled his driveway?"

Dad opened the door and a gust of chilly air and a few snowflakes swirled in. "Mr. Johnson, happy Thanksgiving! Please, come on in," he said to the hunched man standing on the front porch, bundled in a brown trench coat, blue knitted scarf, and fedora pulled low on his forehead.

"Payne, are you sure?" the old man asked gruffly. "If you've changed your mind, I can just go home." Mr. Johnson motioned to his Rolls-Royce, parked in the driveway.

"No minds have changed." Dad smiled and stepped back to make room as Mr. Johnson walked across the threshold and into the house. "EJ, would you please hang up Mr. Johnson's coat?"

EJ tentatively stepped from behind Dad, where she had been hiding. Mr. Johnson looked at her and narrowed his eyes through his glasses—or was he just squinting? Maybe his eyesight wasn't very good.

The old man handed a small brown paper sack to Dad then removed his coat and hat and handed them to EJ. Finally he carefully removed his blue scarf and folded it in half once, twice, three times—as if it were knitted out of unicorn hair or something just as rare—and handed it to EJ as well.

"Make sure that doesn't get wadded up at the bottom of the closet, girl," he said harshly. EJ put the things in the closet, being extra careful that the scarf lay neatly on the top shelf.

"All set? Let's head in, and I'll introduce you to everyone," Dad said.

Mr. Johnson looked uncomfortable as he pulled on the orange floral necktie he'd paired with a slightly wrinkled dark green dress shirt that was tucked into faded brown corduroy pants.

"Good house, Payne," he said to Dad. "Nice and sturdy." Mr. Johnson looked around, apparently inspecting the construction of the house as the men walked from the entryway into the living room.

"Weird," EJ muttered under her breath, following a few steps behind.

Dad introduced Mr. Johnson to Aunt CJ and Isaac, who had just signed off from their video chat with Nana and Pops. When Isaac saw who it was, he bolted to a hiding spot behind the sofa. "Isaac's a little shy, but he'll warm up," Dad said. Aunt CJ was the opposite of shy, and she shook Mr. Johnson's hand warmly and smiled, offering him the best seat in the living room: Dad's recliner.

"Payne, that bag can go into the kitchen with the other food for dinner," Mr. Johnson said, motioning to the paper sack Dad

146

held. "Mother always said not to go to a dinner party empty-handed. I haven't gone to many dinner parties the past few years, but I still remember that."

Dad peered into the bag and pulled an object out. "You know, Mr. Johnson, I do believe four canisters of sour-cream-and-onion Pringles was exactly what our feast was missing," he said, completely sincere. "Thank you."

Mr. Johnson grunted his acknowledgment and leaned back in the recliner, and Dad took the bag to the kitchen. EJ took a seat next to Aunt CJ on the couch and looked warily at the man in Dad's recliner.

"So, Mr. Johnson, did you grow up here in Spooner?" Aunt CJ asked.

"Sure did," Mr. Johnson said. "Born and bred. Met my wife, Ellie—God rest her soul—in 1945 in the second grade at Spooner Elementary."

"Ellie. . .what a nice name," CJ said warmly. EJ tried to signal with her eyes that Mr. Johnson wouldn't like so much interaction, but Aunt CJ didn't seem to notice. "Tell me about Ellie."

EJ admired how easily her aunt spoke to a man who normally didn't care to say more than three words to anyone, let alone carry on an actual human conversation. It was like CJ was a natural-born interviewer.

"My Ellie. . ." Mr. Johnson seemed to soften a bit at the mention of her name. "She had a smile that didn't just light up a room—it could light up the whole town. She was fun and lighthearted and had the sweetest spirit of anyone I ever knew. She was my opposite in so many ways."

Mr. Johnson's eyes shined as he continued to talk about his wife who had passed away nearly a decade ago. He talked about how she loved to travel and how he bought a Rolls-Royce for her so they could drive to see all forty-eight states in style.

"She always said it was too flashy—too expensive," he said, chuckling. "But I told her she was a queen and deserved to travel like one. Anyway, we lived modestly in every other area of our life. She loved clipping coupons from the Sunday paper, and she was a very talented knitter. She even knit the scarf I wore here today."

EJ found herself wishing she had known Ellie Johnson. She sounded lovely. Even Isaac poked his head over the armrest of the couch to watch and listen to Mr. Johnson share his memories of his beloved wife.

"Dinner is served in the great hall, my lords and ladies," Mrs. Winkle announced from the doorway between the living room and kitchen. "Mr. Johnson, it's so good to see you out and about." She smiled at the man in the recliner. "And I *adore* your orange and green color combination today. You match the sweet-potato-green-bean casserole I invented for today's meal."

"Sounds terrible," Mr. Johnson said, making a face. "So terrible it just might be delicious. Kind of like that sweater, Wilma Winkle. . . so hideous that it's strangely beautiful."

"That's what I was going for, dear." Mrs. Winkle smiled and walked into the kitchen, Mr. Johnson following. "Come along, everyone!"

The whole exchange between Mrs. Winkle and Mr. Johnson left EJ entirely confused. "Aunt CJ, what *was* that?" she whispered.

"I think that's what's known as good, old-fashioned *flirting*," CJ said, grinning.

The family sat around the table, a big, delicious-looking turkey on a platter, surrounded by sides: mashed potatoes, gravy, orange-cranberry Jell-O salad, homemade rolls, Mrs. Winkle's new casserole invention, and Mr. Johnson's addition of Pringles, arranged neatly on a serving plate. EJ was finally able to get a look at Mrs. Winkle's handcrafted centerpiece—a pilgrim hat fashioned out of empty paper-towel and toilet-paper rolls.

"What a feast," Dad said, rubbing his hands together in anticipation. "Before we dig in, let's go around the table and share one thing that we're thankful for."

Isaac was thankful that his hair had grown enough that you could hardly tell he had a bald spot. Mrs. Winkle was thankful for the beautiful snow outside her window. Dad was thankful for the food on the table—especially his favorite: mashed potatoes. Mom was thankful for her kids and their unique personalities. EJ was thankful for Bert. CJ was thankful for her safe trip from Chicago to Spooner. Mr. Johnson had to think an extra second or two.

"I don't spend much time being thankful," he said, looking down at his plate. "I guess. . .I guess today I am thankful to be with other people on Thanksgiving. Gruff is good company most of the time, but he's not much for talking."

Dad smiled. "Let's pray." Everyone bowed their heads as Dad began, "Lord, we praise You as the founder of this feast, as the founder of every blessing, and as the founder of our hope of eternity with You. Make us truly thankful every day. It's because of Your Son, Jesus, that we pray these things. Amen."

Dad started a flurry of turkey carving, and plates were filled with a little bit of everything. Isaac tried to load his plate with just a buttered roll and about forty Pringles, but Mom put a stop to that immediately. "The only way I'd let you carb-load like that is if you were running a marathon tomorrow, Isaac," Mom told him, filling his plate with the other food.

EJ sneaked bites of food to Bert, who sat expectantly at her knees. She didn't normally feed him from the table (and technically she wasn't supposed to feed him people food), but Thanksgiving was a special occasion.

Everyone chatted easily over the meal. Mr. Johnson was more animated than EJ could've imagined—even in a daydream—and he even laughed the loudest of anyone at Isaac's knock-knock joke. EJ figured it was just because it was the first time he'd heard it. *Wait till the seventy-eighth time, Mr. Johnson,* she thought.

The big surprise of the meal was that Mrs. Winkle's sweet potato and green bean casserole was actually quite good. And it was Isaac who figured out that a couple of crushed sour cream and onion Pringles on top made it even better.

"You two make a fantastic team," CJ said to Mrs. Winkle and Mr. Johnson, as she sprinkled a handful of Pringle crumbs on her second helping of casserole.

"Team Wink-son!" Isaac shouted, pumping his fist in the air. "Colorful and delicious!"

EJ looked around the table to see general agreement on the faces. Why was everyone encouraging whatever was going on between them?

"Strangest Thanksgiving ever," she whispered to Bert as she slipped him another piece of turkey.

Chapter 13

CHRISTMAS TEA AT 20,000 FEET

Dear Diary,

I'm wearing a dress.

And I'm not happy

about it.

Mom insisted that I

wear it because we're going

to a Christmas tea at a place

called Rosedale Residence. Rosedale is a big

building with apartments where older people live if they

need a little extra help and shouldn't live alone. We go

there sometimes to sing old church songs out of these

books Dad calls him-nalls. (I asked him if there are

her-nalls, and he just laughed. I didn't really know I was

being funny, and I wasn't sure what to do, so I laughed,

too.)

I'm wearing this green velvet Christmas dress that

was Mom's when she was a kid. ("Christmas dresses like

this one don't go out of style," she said. "Yeah right," I

said.) Here are some of the dress's more horrible details: a

white snowflake lace collar that's a little too tight around

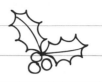

my neck, three red buttons down the front
(purely for decoration), a weirdly high waist,
and a skirt that goes past my knees but not all
the way to the floor, complete with netting underneath
so it poofs out in a not-flattering kind of way.

The one good thing about my outfit today is that the
shoes I was supposed to wear with the dress are too small
for me, so Mom is (reluctantly) letting me wear my
Converse All Stars—the newish black ones that don't look
too ratty. She said that they wouldn't be too noticeable
since I am wearing black tights ("And just try to
remember to keep your ankles crossed and tucked under
your chair," she said). If the rest of me is uncomfortable,
at least my feet will feel normal.

The other thing is that I'm a little nervous about
being around old people, Diary. And when I say old, I
mean ancient. It's safe to assume these women will be
cheek-pinchers who wear too much perfume.

Here goes nothing.

EJ

EJ sat bolt upright in a stiff-backed chair at a table elegantly set for tea for three: a white lace tablecloth; delicate China teacups, saucers, and small plates that had tiny clusters of holly leaves and berries painted around the edges; and a two-tiered tray of small chicken salad croissant sandwiches and finger desserts. It all looked so fancy that EJ was afraid even just looking at something too hard would make it shatter.

Soft Christmas melodies played in the background as EJ focused on keeping her hands in her lap and her ankles crossed under her chair. She looked around the room at the other girls sitting at similar-looking small tables. She saw the McCallisters at one table, CoraLee adjusting the pair of long silk gloves she was wearing. Katy sat next to her, looking miserable in a frilly, yellow dress that looked like an oversized ballerina tutu. In the corner of the room, she found Macy smiling and waving at her in a pretty red-and-white drop-waist dress that looked like it was from the 1920s. Making sure no breakables were nearby, EJ raised her right hand and waved back.

Soon moms started coming into the room, each with a female Rosedale resident on her arm. The elderly women were dressed just as fancy as the girls waiting at their tables, and many of them looked like they had just gotten their hair and makeup done especially for the Christmas tea.

Mom escorted a tiny woman with short blazing-red hair, lipstick, and fingernail polish to match. She wore a dark blue jacket that had small Christmas bulb ornaments embroidered on the collar, a black knee-length skirt that flared out at the bottom, and she carried a small black beaded clutch.

EJ stood and pulled out the chair for their tea companion as she approached the table.

"EJ, this is Mrs. Rice," Mom said. "Mrs. Rice, this is my ten-year-old daughter, Emma Jean. But we call her EJ."

"Emma Jean is a fine name, but I like EJ even more." Mrs. Rice's eyes sparkled as she shook EJ's hand with a surprisingly firm (but gentle) handshake for as old as she looked. "Please, both of you, call me Alice."

"I'm glad to meet you, Alice," EJ said as she helped the woman scoot her chair to the table before sitting down across from her. Alice's smiling eyes and easy manner made EJ less nervous.

Mom, wearing a pretty knee-length black dress and a Christmas-red shrug, sat in the third seat at the table. "Shall I pour, Alice?" she asked.

"Oh yes, thank you," Alice answered, placing her linen napkin neatly in her lap. "I have the experience necessary for serving, but I'm afraid I'm a little too clumsy anymore."

"Experience?" EJ asked, following Alice's example of putting the napkin in her lap. "Did you serve tea for a living before you retired, Mrs. Ri—er—Alice?"

Alice's eyes danced as she watched Mom pour steaming amber-colored liquid into her teacup. "It was one part of my job. I was an airline stewardess for ten years before I got married and stayed home to raise my children," she said.

"Whoa, really?" EJ asked. "So have you been all over the world?"

"If a city had an international airport in the 1950s, yes, I have probably been there," Alice said. "And back then being a stewardess was almost as glamorous as you can imagine."

Alice retrieved a picture from the clutch she held in her lap. "This is me in my uniform in 1953. I am barely twenty years old here—so young and with so many stars in my eyes."

EJ took the old picture carefully and studied it. What she saw was a much younger-looking version of a smiling Alice in a tailored jacket and pencil skirt that fell just past her knees. There was a little pin in the shape of an airliner on one lapel, and a beautiful rose pinned to the other. A small hat sat just so on her head—a pair of high heels on her feet.

"Is it true," Mom began, "that back then, traveling by plane was more than just getting from point A to point B?"

"It's absolutely true, Tabby," Alice said. "Traveling was an event. People dressed in their Sunday best, and it was our job as stewardesses to make sure they had all the comforts of home, even 20,000 feet up in the air."

"Cool." EJ sighed.

"But we did more than just serve coffee, tea, food, and get blankets and pillows for our guests," Alice continued. "We were trained and ready for any situation that might arise on the plane so that everyone arrived at their destinations safely. We just got to be pretty while doing it!" She laughed.

The three sipped tea, ate chicken salad sandwiches, and chatted happily about this and that—EJ's favorite subject in school, family Christmas plans, the nativity pageant at church, the weather.

"EJ, hon, would you take our teapot to the serving cart and refill it with hot water?" Mom asked, holding the China teapot out to her. "So we can have a little more tea to go with our dessert?"

"You want *me* to carry *that*?" EJ asked, a little shocked Mom would trust her with such a task. "I'm not sure that's a good idea."

"You'll do fine, dear," Alice assured her, placing a wrinkled hand over her smaller, smooth one. "How else will you be able to practice for your future career as a stewardess. . .or what do they call them today? Flight attendants?"

"I'd rather be a stewardess in the 1950s," EJ said. "Well, except for those high heels. How did you stay upright on a moving plane, Alice?"

"With a lot of practice." Alice smiled. "And after I retired from my stewardess job, I vowed I'd never wear a pair of them again. Now I'm all about comfort over style. See?" Alice stuck an orthopedic-shoed foot out from under the table to show EJ.

"Me, too, Alice." EJ smiled and showed off her beloved All Stars.

"You are like two peas in a pod," Mom said, laughing. "Now, EJ, our desserts need some tea before our plane arrives at our destination. . . ."

"Yes, ma'am." EJ took the teapot with both hands and walked toward the serving cart.

It had been a while since EJ had worked a trans-Atlantic flight that was as full as this one. With guests filling every seat, she is on her toes to make sure everyone has everything they want. As she arrives in the plane's galley, she sets the teapot down for a second to catch her breath.

"EJ, isn't this so fun?" Macy stood at the serving cart, pouring hot water into her teapot from an insulated carafe. "The lady Mom and I are sitting with used to dance with the Rockettes at Radio City Music Hall in New York!"

"Mine was an airline stewardess in the 1950s, who's been all over the globe," EJ said, looking over the rest of the room and wondering what other amazing stories were being shared. "I have to admit that this Christmas-tea thing is way better than I thought it'd be."

"See you afterward?" Macy asked, concentrating on holding her teapot now full of hot water.

"Yeah, see you," EJ responded. She turned back to the serving cart.

Now that the in-flight meal has been cleared away, EJ relaxes a bit, knowing she's in the homestretch until the plane lands safely in London. EJ goes over orders in her head: the couple in row four asked for sugar for their tea, the businessman in row eight wants creamer for his coffee, and the mom in row nine requested milk for her young son.

She loads her serving apron with plenty of sugar packets, powdered creamer, and a carton of milk for the little boy, picks up the refilled teapot, and heads back to her section, a smile on her lips.

On her way through the rows of seats, her eyes scan back and forth, looking for anyone who may need something. She spots an empty teacup on a lady's tray table and politely asks, "More tea, ma'am?"

"Yes, thank you," the elderly woman replies. She's traveling in style, dressed in a particularly fancy fur-collared jacket. "And do you have any sugar?"

"Here you are, ma'am." EJ expertly pours the tea and sets five sugar packets on the tray table. "May I do anything else for you?"

The woman looks up at EJ and smiles. "Five sugar packets—a woman after my own heart!" she exclaims. "You must like your tea the same way I do—sweet enough to pour on pancakes if we run out of syrup."

EJ and the woman laugh. But a second later, the woman makes a little gasping noise and starts to cough a deep, rattling cough in her chest.

"Ma'am? Ma'am?" EJ sets the teapot down quickly and crouches down next to the woman. "Are you all right?"

EJ snapped out of her daydream as the woman in the fur collar took a ragged breath and began to cough again. EJ looked around frantically, trying to see who this woman was sitting with, but the other chairs at the table were empty. As the woman coughed, she pointed to a thin plastic tube under her nose. EJ had seen one of those on TV—an oxygen tube! EJ got on all fours and looked under the woman's chair and spotted a small oxygen tank.

"Please, someone, get a nurse!" EJ yelled from the floor. "I think there's something wrong with this woman's oxygen tank!" She heard some quick footsteps and what sounded like a mom voice say, "Hold on. . .someone will be right here to help you, ma'am."

As the woman continued to cough above her, EJ found where the tube attached to the oxygen tank and followed it with her eyes along the floor until she saw that the tube was lodged under one of the legs of the woman's chair. The weight of it must have been pinching off the oxygen supply!

EJ popped up to her feet and grasped the back of the woman's chair. "Hold on," she said as she pulled the chair back a few inches. She dropped to her knees again and gently eased the length of the tube up from the floor and draped it across the woman's lap. Within a few moments, her coughing eased a bit and she was able to breathe more normally.

A nurse wearing red-and-green scrubs ran up to the woman a few seconds later. "Evelyn, are you okay?" she asked, rubbing the woman's back and checking her oxygen supply. "What happened?"

"Her oxygen tube got stuck under her chair, and I don't think she could get the air she needed," EJ said, picking her teapot up again so she had something to hold.

Just then Mrs. McCallister and her two girls rushed up to the table.

"Evelyn, are you okay?" Mrs. McCallister looked genuinely concerned. "We were just walking back from the restroom and someone told us you were in some kind of breathing distress. . . ."

"I'll be fine, Liz." Evelyn had caught up on just enough air to get the words out. "Thanks to this quick-thinking young woman." She nodded toward EJ and smiled.

"EJ, once again you're here right when we need you," Mrs. McCallister said. "Thank you." Katy beamed at EJ, and even CoraLee looked mildly impressed with EJ's skills.

"Well done, stewardess-in-training!" EJ heard Alice's smiling voice call behind her. She turned around to see the redheaded lady giving her a thumbs-up from her seat at their table across the room.

After making one last check to make sure Evelyn was okay, EJ went back to her table with Mom and Alice.

"I'm proud of you, EJ," Mom said, leaning over to give her daughter a squeeze on the shoulder.

"We saw the whole thing," Alice said excitedly, digging through her purse. "You might be the fastest trainee in the history of the airline, but you displayed such ability, courage, and quick thinking today, that you deserve this. . . ."

Alice held out her hand, palm up, to reveal an airplane-shaped gold pin. "The very same one I'm wearing in the picture," she said.

"You're giving it to me?" EJ asked, wide-eyed.

"It's for you," Alice said, pinning it on the lace collar of EJ's dress. "I am a dreamer just like you, EJ. Someday—very soon—it'll be time to stretch your wings and fly."

EJ looked down at the gleaming airplane pin on her chest and thought she had never seen anything quite so special.

Chapter 14

WHAT THE ANGEL OVERHEARD

December 23

Dear Diary,

After eight weeks of torturous practices where I had to watch CoraLee in the starring role of Mary that I was obviously destined to play, tonight is the dress rehearsal for the Christmas play.

I kind of can't wait for it all to be over.

There are, however, two things that will make the nativity pageant bearable:

Angel flight: At last week's rehearsal, Dad rigged up this crazy-looking harness that he told me was part of my costume. It seemed weird and like nothing I had ever seen an angel wear, but I stepped into it and he tightened all the straps around my legs and waist. Just as I was about to ask what it was for, Dad hooked it to a rope hanging from the ceiling on the stage, pulled firmly on another rope, and I rose up two feet off the floor like I was flying! Dad said the surprised shock on my face was outstanding. (Alice told me at the Christmas tea that I was going to fly sometime soon, but I don't think this is what she had in mind. . . .) He asked if I wanted to go higher, and I said yes, so he pulled more and up I went—into the perfect spot high above the stage for an angel to proclaim "Glory to God in the highest heaven!" It also gives me an excellent view of anyone who might be taking a snooze in the audience. Cool, huh?

Angel glitter: Normally I'm not allowed to wear makeup, but Mom is going to let me wear gold glitter eye shadow, shimmer lip gloss, and glittery nail polish for the pageant. ("The Bible says that when the angel appeared to the shepherds, the glory of the Lord shined down. Who knows? Maybe God's glory is gold and sparkly," Mom said.) Obviously I'm usually a no-frills kind of girl, Diary, but I'm the Christmas angel pronouncing the birth of the Savior of the world, so like Mrs. Winkle said at Thanksgiving, "Go big or go home!"

As always, I bring you good tidings of great joy,

EJ

"Ready, EJ?" Dad looked up at EJ from his spot backstage, the rope attached to the rigging and the angel harness in his hand.

EJ looked down from the wooden platform she stood on, already a good eight feet off the ground. She tugged on the harness under her angel robe, and it felt secure.

"Ready for launch," EJ whispered. Dad slowly pulled down on the rope.

EJ held her breath as she felt the rope start to pull up. She liked being up in the air during the angel scene, but that moment just before her toes left the platform, it always felt a little like her stomach would fall out and roll around on the floor.

CoraLee walks the length of the backstage, preparing for her next entrance. Suddenly she steps on something squishy and looks down on the floor.

"What is this?" she asks no one in particular.

"It's my stomach. . .it fell out this time." EJ dangles from above, grinning down at CoraLee. "Pretty cool, huh?"

CoraLee screams as she runs off the stage, up the aisle of the auditorium, and out the door. A distraught Michael Draper runs after her.

"Well, it looks like we'll need a new Mary and Joseph," Mrs. Winkle says from her spot on the front pew where she is watching the dress rehearsal. "EJ. . .Cory, are you two up for it?"

The few seconds of the daydream had been enough to distract EJ, and she was now hovering ten feet above the stage. A spotlight swiveled, illuminating her in a beam of bright light, her cue to start her lines. "Hey, you shepherds down there, don't be afraid—I'm not going to hurt you."

Mrs. Winkle had let the fourth graders write their own lines for the pageant (as part of the "creative process of the art of theater," she'd said).

The shepherds and the preschool sheep stared up at EJ, looking genuinely impressed at how high the rigging held her. The effect made them look like they were awestruck by the glory of the angel above them. (EJ thought that was a good thing because none of them were very convincing actors.)

"I know you've never seen anything like me before," EJ continued. "But I'm a messenger, sent here from God, and I have good news that will change your lives and the lives of everyone in the world!"

The lights on the entire stage brightened as the angel choir emerged through a curtain and filed onto a set of risers directly below EJ. She noticed a couple angels look up nervously—apparently still not trusting that the rigging would hold her. One particularly tiny first-grade angel tripped on the hem of her robe, and she took a face-dive off the bottom step of the risers. Luckily, a nearby third-grade angel caught her by the back of her robe before she could fall flat out.

"Whoops! Nice save, Jared!" Mrs. Winkle called from her seat in the empty auditorium. "Hannah, we'll make sure your robe is hemmed before tomorrow night, dear. Keep going, EJ!"

"Earlier tonight, in a stable in Bethlehem, a tiny baby was born. But he isn't just *any* baby," EJ said, delivering the lines with all the passion she could muster. "He's the Savior of the world— the Messiah you've been waiting for!"

One of the preschool sheep *baa*'ed excitedly. Will Bowers poked her with his shepherd staff to shut her up.

"Will! No poking!" Mrs. Winkle's usually smiley voice turned a little teachery. "Do it again, and I'll take away your staff."

"Sorry, Mrs. Winkle," Will said, looking guilty.

"Mrs. Winkle, I was just excited that Jesus was born," said the little sheep who had received the poke.

"Yes, yes, darling—it was perfect!" Mrs. Winkle said. "All you sheep—and you shepherds, too—get excited when the angel announces that the Messiah has been born. Take it back one line please, EJ. And. . .action!"

"He's the Savior of the world—the Messiah you've been waiting for!" EJ repeated.

A chorus of *baa*'s from the sheep and excited grunts from the shepherds followed.

"Here's how you'll know it's him," EJ continued. "The baby will be snuggled in strips of cloth and his mother used the manger filled with soft hay for *his bed.*"

EJ emphasized the last two words to cue the angels to join her on the next line. In one voice, they said: "Glory to God in the highest heaven, and peace on earth to all men!"

"And women!" the tiny angel named Hannah piped up.

"You're right—women, too," Mrs. Winkle said, the smile back in her voice. "Keep that in tomorrow night, Hannah-girl!"

The music for the angel choir song started, and the spotlight dimmed on EJ. As the cherubs sang a little-kid version of "Angels We Have Heard on High," the rope on the rigging lowered EJ down to her place on the platform. Her part in the pageant was over, but she had to stay on the platform until the whole rehearsal was done because she couldn't get out of the harness herself.

With her feet firmly planted on the platform, she gave Dad the thumbs-up signal so he knew she had landed safely. He waved back then turned around to help Leslie Sattler keep the nativity animals occupied until it was their turn to go back onstage.

EJ tugged a little slack in the rope and sat on the platform, her feet dangling over the edge. Then she pulled Mom's well-worn paperback copy of *Little Women* out of her angel robe and began to read about Jo March and the play she and her three sisters put on in the attic of their house. *Maybe I should write my own plays,* EJ thought. *Then I could always give myself the biggest roles.*

She was just getting to the part in chapter three where Jo meets the neighbor boy named Laurie at a New Year's Eve party when she heard two girls' voices below her. Squinting in the dim light, she saw that it was CoraLee and Katy, both in their nativity costumes. Apparently they didn't realize EJ was still on the platform.

> **CoraLee:** "Come on, Katy. . .please stop crying. You have to go onstage in a minute, and the donkey at the manger scene can't be sobbing in the background. You'll distract from my big scene."

Oh brother, EJ thought, rolling her eyes.

> **Katy:** *(sniff)* "But, CoraLee, Mom said we aren't having Christmas this year. Doesn't that make you sad?"
> **CoraLee:** "Yeah, it does. Sad and disappointed and mad all at the same time. But Dad lost his job four months ago, and that's a long time to go without money. I heard Mom and Dad talking about it the other night—we might have to move out of our house if he doesn't get a job soon."
> **Katy:** *(crying)* "So. . .no Christmas *and* we're going to be homeless?"
> **CoraLee:** *(hugging Katy)* "No, we won't be homeless, Katy. It'll all work out."
> **Katy:** "How do you know?"
> **CoraLee:** "I just do. Listen, you'd better go over with the other nativity animals. How are you going to be the best, most amazing nativity scene donkey in the history of church pageants if you miss your cue?"
> **Katy:** *(wiping her eyes on the back of her donkey hooves)* "I do make a pretty great donkey."

Katy gave a convincing donkey bray and walked toward the side of the stage where Dad and Leslie were still trying to herd the nativity animals, who were getting rowdier by the minute. EJ tried to process what she'd just heard. She had no idea that Mr. McCallister had lost his job or that the family was having money problems.

EJ looked down again and saw CoraLee standing still, holding the baby Jesus (a doll wrapped up tight in a white cloth) close.

"Hey, God, it's me. . .CoraLee McCallister," EJ heard CoraLee say quietly. "I told Katy it'll all work out, but the truth is, I need Your help. It seems like Mom and Dad are fighting about money all the time now. And I'm afraid our problems are even worse than they've told me."

EJ felt guilty listening in on CoraLee's private conversation with God, but trapped on the platform, she just decided to keep quiet rather than let CoraLee know she'd been there, listening the whole time.

"Jesus, You did so many amazing miracles in the Bible, so please do another one now. Not for me—for Katy," CoraLee said. "I am asking for You to take care of us. Please make it all work out. I know You can. Amen."

EJ watched CoraLee push her way through the heavy backstage curtains to take her place onstage for the finale. EJ's mind spun as she replayed everything she had just heard. Was this another one of those "EJ's in the right place at the right time" kind of moments? And if she was there for a reason, stuck up on that platform to overhear CoraLee and Katy, what could she *actually* do? It's not like she had a job for Mr. McCallister or enough money she could give to the family to help them keep their house. . . .

Suddenly from the side of the stage, EJ heard Isaac's distinctive elephant trumpet noise followed by a stampede of tiny feet storming onto the stage. "Whoa!" she heard Dad shout, and a half second later, she felt the harness yank her up off the platform.

"Heeeeeey!" was all EJ could get out, so surprised that she lost her grip of Mom's copy of *Little Women* and it went sailing to the floor below. The next second, EJ saw the stage, auditorium, and backstage on a loop as the rigging spun her around and around, high above Mary, Joseph, the shepherds, the three wise guys, the angel choir, and all the animals. Dozens of eyes stared up at her, and while EJ normally would enjoy being the center of attention, she was feeling dizzier with each spin.

"Daaad?" Even just opening her mouth to say the word might've been a bad idea, she decided, covering her mouth with her hand.

"EJ, hold on, honey!" Dad called from backstage. "Sorry, Mrs. Winkle. . .minor technical difficulties. A herd of wild nativity animals got loose. It won't happen tomorrow."

EJ heard a click and felt the rigging balance itself out—she slowly stopped spinning and came to a halt. The kids onstage burst into applause. EJ felt too ill to try to bow, so she smiled instead.

"Well, that was certainly. . .exciting," Mrs. Winkle called from her seat. "I do like the idea of having you back onstage for the finale, though, EJ. What do you think—do you want to stay up there and sing 'Silent Night' with everyone else?"

"Sure thing, Mrs. Winkle!" EJ said, happy to get a few more minutes onstage.

As the Paynes piled out of the minivan when they got home from dress rehearsal, Mom pointed at something on their front porch.

"I'm not expecting anything to be delivered today," Mom said. "EJ, why don't you go see what it is?"

EJ found a brown paper grocery bag, filled with food—canned

soup, canned mixed vegetables, canned peaches, two boxed dinners, and a box of instant mashed potatoes. Sitting on top of the food was an envelope. EJ tore it open and read the note, scrawled in shaky handwriting:

> *Payne children,*
>
> *A few weeks ago, you came to my door to ask for a food donation for the poor. I didn't react very well to you, and (as you are aware) I didn't give you anything.*
>
> *When you and your dad came and shoveled my driveway and invited me to Thanksgiving, I was skeptical. I still thought maybe you Paynes wanted something from me or that the preacher just wanted me to give money to the church. But then I came to Thanksgiving. You welcomed me into your house and convinced me that there are still good people in the world. You Paynes are good people.*
>
> *And, well, I decided I want to try to be a better person. Show more kindness. Help when I can. And here's the start of that. I realize your food drive at school might be over by now, but there are always people in need, and you will know what to do with this.*
>
> *Sincerely,*
> *Lester Johnson*

EJ stuffed the note into her coat pocket and heaved the grocery bag by its handles. Mr. Johnson having a change of heart—who would've thought?

"Mom. . .Dad. . .check this out!" she called as she walked through the door from the garage into the kitchen. "Mr. Johnson left a note and these groceries on the porch—for the food drive."

EJ set the bag on the counter and handed Mom the envelope from her coat pocket. Mom read it silently and handed it to Dad, who read it and muttered quietly, "Well, I never in a million years would've believed it. . . ."

EJ thought Dad's reaction was a little over the top. "It's really great that Mr. Johnson decided to be less of a grouch, Dad, but it's just a few groceries—"

Dad handed EJ the envelope. "Look again," he said, his eyes bright.

EJ folded open the flap of the envelope and saw what she overlooked the first time: a check made out to the Spooner Food Pantry for $10,000.

"Wooow!" EJ said, amazed. "I bet that check could buy enough SpaghettiOs to fill a swimming pool!"

"Oooo, yum!" Isaac looked up from the kitchen table where he was drawing a picture of (what else) a T-Rex. "I want to swim in *that* pool!"

"This money will help out so many people in the area," Mom said, gazing at the check. "But. . .ten-thousand dollars? Mr. Johnson? Who knew he had that kind of money?"

"Wait. What name did he sign on the note?" Dad checked the paper in his hand. "Lester. . .Lester Johnson. . . Why does that name sound familiar?"

Dad pulled his phone out of his pocket and did a quick Internet search. A few moments later, he looked up at Mom and EJ with a big grin on his face.

"Lester Johnson. . .our Mr. Johnson," Dad said. "Our neighborhood grump. . .the man with the soft spot for cats, who thinks Isaac's joke is hilarious. . ."

"Hey, it's funny!" Isaac cut in.

"Daaad, get on with it," EJ said. "Who is Mr. Johnson?"

". . .is none other than Lester Johnson—the owner of Lester's Car Mart. Actually, he owns a dozen Lester's Car Marts in Wisconsin and Minnesota."

"As in, 'Let Lester make you a deal' from the TV commercials?" EJ asked.

"Sure is!" Dad said. "He is a very wealthy man."

EJ's mind spun. She wasn't sure how, but this *had* to be part of the plan—the big, important something that she was supposed to do. Now she just needed someone to help her connect all the dots. . . .

"Dad, there's something else I need to tell you," EJ said. "Something that I overheard at dress rehearsal. . ."

Chapter 15

CODE CHRISTMAS

December 24

Dear Diary,

You know, I always thought I'd be secretly happy if something sort of bad happened to CoraLee. I mean, she isn't exactly nice to me. But then I found out about her dad losing his job and the struggles they're having. And when I heard her pray, I actually felt sorry for her. . .so sorry that I wanted to do something to help. But what could I do to actually make a difference? Empty out all $39.83 from my savings account at the Spooner Credit Union? I'm only ten, but even I know that won't go very far.

Dad always says there's no such thing as a coincidence—that events don't just randomly happen, but there's a purpose for everything. Last night after rehearsal, we found Mr. Johnson's food donation and note. And that's when the pieces of what we're calling "Code Christmas" started falling into place.

I wish I had more time to tell you what's happening tonight, Diary, but it's just about an hour till the curtain rises on the Vine Street Community Church Christmas pageant—and I still need to get in my angel flight harness. I can hear Isaac practicing his goat sounds in his bedroom next door, but after the dress rehearsal fiasco, I have a sneaking suspicion that he's going to try to work in an elephant trumpet noise at just the right moment to steal the show.

My whole life I've known that I'm destined for big things, so I've been preparing for that "someday." But the truth is that there are big things for me to do now as a kid, here in the boringest place on the planet. And tonight, I know for sure what I'm supposed to do.

More later, Diary.
Time for this angel to fly!
EJ

EJ spread her arms wide and wiggled her fingers in the spotlight, hoping the audience would notice her gold-sparkle-painted fingernails. The entire stage below was filled with kids for the finale—all (including EJ) singing "Silent Night." The audience seemed completely wrapped up in the precious Christmas scene taking place in front of them.

Everything had gone off without a hitch. Well, almost. . . During the "Away in a Manger" scene, Joseph accidentally kicked over the manger and sent the baby Jesus doll rolling across the stage. Isaac broke character from being a goat and ever-so-helpfully picked up the doll and carried it back to Mary, who looked horrified by the whole scene. "It's okay, I'm a goat, but I'm also a doctor," Isaac told CoraLee, who snatched the baby back from him. "Newborns are pretty rubbery when they come out," he explained to the audience, who laughed and clapped for the goat who saved the day. Satisfied that all was well, Isaac dropped back to all fours, gave an ear-piercing "meeehhh!" and crawled back to his spot with the other animals.

After the final notes of "Silent Night," the audience clapped and cheered. Then they stood and clapped some more. EJ decided the part of the angel wasn't so bad. There were lots of smiling faces looking up at her, some waving and others pointing—obviously impressed with her ability to play a convincing messenger from God from so high in the air.

A few minutes later, everyone was in the fellowship hall enjoying Christmas cookies and punch. EJ had just bitten into a stocking-shaped iced cookie when she saw Mrs. Winkle guiding a rather uncomfortable-looking Mr. Johnson through the crowd, toward Mr. and Mrs. McCallister.

Here we go, EJ thought. *Code Christmas—phase one.*

She shoved the rest of the cookie into her mouth and took a

gulp of punch to wash it down. Then, weaving through the crowd, she found the perfect hiding spot behind a nearby Christmas tree to listen in on the conversation that was happening between Mrs. Winkle, Mr. Johnson, and the McCallisters.

"CoraLee and Katy did absolutely wonderfully in the pageant," Mrs. Winkle said to Mr. and Mrs. McCallister. "I'm so proud of both of them—as I'm sure you are, too."

"Oh yes, the whole thing was just perfect, Wilma," Mrs. McCallister said. "Thank you for all the work you put into the play."

"You know I'm not much for plays, Wilma," Mr. Johnson said. "But this one definitely had your special. . .pizzazz."

"Oh, now, Mr. Johnson," Mrs. Winkle said, blushing a little.

EJ rolled her eyes.

"Mr. McCallister, have you met Mr. Johnson?" Mrs. Winkle asked. "He lives in my neighborhood—just a couple of blocks over."

"No, I don't believe I've had the pleasure." Mr. McCallister stuck out his hand to Mr. Johnson. "Ben McCallister."

"Nice to meet you, McCallister," Mr. Johnson said, shaking the younger man's hand. "What do you do for a living?"

"Let's let the men talk shop, dear," Mrs. Winkle said to Mrs. McCallister. "Shall we go get a refill on our punch?"

Mrs. McCallister looked helplessly at her husband, as Mrs. Winkle took her elbow and steered her toward the punch bowl.

"Well, I'm in sales," Mr. McCallister said, fiddling with his empty coffee cup.

Mr. Johnson nodded. "What kind of sales are you in, Ben?"

Mr. McCallister cleared his throat nervously.

"Well. . .currently. . .I'm between sales positions," Mr. McCallister said. "But until four months ago I sold dairy farming equipment—but then the company I worked for went bankrupt."

"I see," Mr. Johnson grunted. "These are mighty challenging times."

Mr. McCallister nodded.

Mr. Johnson eyed the younger man, as if he were sizing him up right there on the spot.

"McCallister, you don't know me, and I don't know much about you," Mr. Johnson said. "But I own a business—one that you've probably heard of. My nephew runs the day-to-day now so that I can stay home with my cat, but I still have a say in what goes on there." Mr. Johnson handed Mr. McCallister a business card.

Mr. McCallister looked up from the business card. "You— you're 'Let Lester make you a deal' Johnson," Mr. McCallister stammered. "Of Lester's Car Mart!"

"I've aged a bit since my days on the commercials, haven't I?" Mr. Johnson chuckled. "Son, to be honest, someone told me about your situation and I did a little homework on you. What I found out is that you were one of the top sales associates at your previous job. And from what I can tell, you are an honest man and a hard worker."

EJ smiled from behind the Christmas tree, knowing what was coming next.

"All that to say, I'd like you to come in and interview for a sales position for us," Mr. Johnson said. "If you're interested, that is."

"*If* I'm interested?" Mr. McCallister couldn't have looked happier than if he had just won the lottery. "Yes, sir. I'm interested. And honored to be considered." Mr. McCallister took Mr. Johnson's hand and pumped it enthusiastically.

"Just get in touch with the corporate office on December 26," Mr. Johnson said. "They'll be expecting your call."

"First thing December 26—will do," Mr. McCallister said. "But, I am curious, Mr. Johnson. We didn't tell anyone outside the family that I was out of work. Who was it that told you?"

"I've learned a lot in the past few weeks, McCallister," Mr.

Johnson said. "One thing I've learned is that there are still decent, kind people in this world. And a few of them might even be angels in disguise." Without warning, and without anyone else seeing, Mr. Johnson looked straight at EJ in her hiding spot and gave an approving nod. EJ grinned and gave him a thumbs-up.

"Merry Christmas, McCallister," Mr. Johnson said gruffly and walked away.

"Merry Christmas, Mr. Johnson!" Mr. McCallister called after him. "And thank you!"

Mrs. McCallister walked up to her husband, a cup of punch in each hand. "What was that all about, Ben?" she asked. "Your face looks flushed."

"The beginning of an answer to our prayers, Liz!" Mr. McCallister said. "An answer—out of *nowhere*! Let's go find the girls—I have great news to share."

Code Christmas—phase one: check! EJ thought.

★

Three hours later—at almost 11 p.m.—the Paynes were loaded up in the minivan, sitting in their driveway making last-minute preparations for phase two.

"Okay, guys, do we all know what's happening?" EJ asked.

"I'm in charge of the box of food," Dad said.

"I'm in charge of the box of presents," Mom said.

"I'm the lookout and in charge of Bert," Isaac said.

Bert, who was sitting in Isaac's lap, barked his agreement.

"And I'm in charge of the note—and ringing the doorbell," EJ said.

EJ looked around at her family—each dressed in black from head to toe as part of the covert plan of phase two. It had been pretty simple to keep phase one a secret from the McCallisters, but phase two was going to be more of a risk.

Dad turned around in the driver's seat to look at EJ and Isaac. "Listen, you two, are you sure this is what you want to do?" he asked. "I think giving Christmas to the McCallisters is absolutely fantastic, but it's going to mean that our Christmas won't be the same as usual tomorrow."

"No presents, no ham dinner with the fixings," Mom said. "Are you *sure* you're okay with that?"

EJ looked in the back of the minivan where she saw the makings of what would've been their family Christmas. Sure, it'd be fun to open up presents, and Mom's Christmas dinner was one of the best all year. But the opportunity to surprise the McCallisters with Christmas—when they didn't expect to have Christmas at all— seemed somehow even better and more important. EJ wasn't really sure how or why, but this whole thing with giving, with showing kindness to others, was kind of addictive.

"Dad. . .Mom, this is how we live out our faith," EJ said. "This is what I *want* to do. It's important."

"Yeah—phase two!" Isaac said. "It's like we're the opposite of robbers!"

Dad started up the minivan. "All right, Paynes. We're really doing it," he said, pulling out of their driveway.

On the ride to the McCallisters' house, EJ unfolded the note she had written to read it one last time:

> *To the McCallister Family:*
> *I didn't mean to find out that Mr. McCallister lost his job. I also didn't mean to find out that you don't have money for Christmas this year. I know you didn't want other people to know, maybe because you were embarrassed.*

But Christmas is about hope, and Christmas is about the possibility of something better. Christmas is about God taking care of us. And in another, smaller way, I think this Christmas He sent me to help you. To help give you hope that next year will be better than this year.

So please accept this Christmas from me and my family. We hope it makes your holiday extra special.

An Angel in Disguise

A few minutes later, Dad pulled the minivan along the curb, headlights off, half a block from the darkened McCallister house.

"That's a good sign," Dad said. "It looks like they're in bed."

Mom handed out red Santa hats—adult-size for her and Dad, kid-size for EJ and Isaac, and a little dog-size hat, complete with an elastic chin strap for Bert. "We need a little holiday fun to go with our black uniforms," she explained.

Silently, they got out of the minvan, leaving the doors open for a quick escape. With presents, food, and note in hand, they tiptoed their way toward the front porch.

The Payne family knows their orders from the home office: deliver the package at the drop, undetected. They're fourth- and fifth-generation spies, so tonight's secret mission should be pretty simple.

As they approach the drop point, Dad silently motions to Isaac to hide behind a row of shrubbery. This will be his lookout spot for the duration and their rendezvous point after the mission is completed. Isaac picks up the family pet (also a super spy in his own right) and darts toward the shrubs, as silent as a shadow.

Mom nods toward the porch and the three remaining spies move as one toward the spot, now less than twenty feet from the goal.

Suddenly, an outside floodlight bursts on, exposing the spies in the driveway.

"Motion lights!" Dad whispers. "This way!"

The trio ducks and sprints into the dark area of the front yard, their hearts racing. They hold their breath, waiting to see if anyone inside will come out to see what tripped the motion sensor. After a few tense moments, the light clicks off again. No sign of anyone inside.

Mom nods toward the porch, and they start again, more cautious this time.

After what seems like an eternity, they make it to the front porch. Mom and Dad set their packages down and give EJ the all-clear signal. She nods at them, and they take off toward the rendezvous point behind the shrubbery.

Now comes the most important part—the part reserved for super spy EJ Payne herself—the alert.

EJ watched Mom and Dad until they were hidden with Isaac behind the shrubs. Her heart pounded in her ears. Any moment the front porch light could flip on, and she could get caught by any of the McCallisters.

"Don't get scared, you've got this," she whispered.

Taking one final deep breath, she set the note in the middle of the welcome mat and rang the doorbell. The sound of the bell pierced through the silence of the cold Christmas Eve, making her jump. But the jump was all she needed to take off like lightning, running and nearly tripping off the top step of the porch. Luckily, she regained her footing through the snow and hurled herself through the shrubs, out of sight, just as the front door opened.

Mr. McCallister stuck his head out, looking confused.

"There's nobody there," he said to Mrs. McCallister as she emerged in the doorway, tying a robe around her waist. "Wait, what's this?" Mr. McCallister picked up the note and started reading.

Mrs. McCallister peered into the boxes on the porch. "Ben, what. . . ?"

CoraLee and Katy, awoken by the doorbell, appeared in the doorway, rubbing their eyes and yawning. "Dad, what's going on?" CoraLee asked.

Mr. McCallister laughed after he read the note. "What a night this has been, girls!" he said. "Mr. Johnson was right—there's an angel looking out for us. It seems we're going to have Christmas after all!" He squinted, looking out into the darkness, and as an afterthought shouted, "Hey, if you can hear me out there—thank you! You've given us a lot more than Christmas today!"

"Yeah, thanks!" Katy shouted.

There was a lot of ooing and ahhing over the contents of the boxes as the McCallisters took everything inside.

When the Paynes heard the door shut, they all breathed a little easier. They walked quietly back to the minivan under a clear sky filled with stars.

"That might've been the coolest thing I've ever done," Dad said once the minivan doors were shut and it was safe to talk.

"Code Christmas, phase two—check!" EJ said, smiling.

"I made the best lookout," Isaac said. "We didn't get caught, so that means I did good."

"Very true, buddy," Mom said. "So now that it's almost Christmas and we just gave ours away, we officially have nothing to do tomorrow. . . ."

"What are you suggesting?" Dad asked.

"I say we head over to Mel's All-Night Diner and have a midnight breakfast," Mom said. "Pancakes, french toast, eggs, waffles. . .and what do you kids say to sausage *and* bacon?"

"Yes and YES!" Isaac shouted. Bert barked his agreement.

"We Paynes do love our breakfast meats," EJ said, thinking that all this secrecy gave her an extra-big appetite.

"To Mel's Diner, it is!" Dad said. "This just might be the start of a new tradition."

Dear Diary,

Today was the very best Christmas ever.

Of course, it started with the best midnight breakfast I've ever had (okay, okay, it's the *only* midnight breakfast I've ever had). You might think that Mel wouldn't want people to come to his restaurant on Christmas Eve, but he was so happy to have us that he led in singing Christmas carols the whole time he was making the food—a lot of food. My absolute favorite are Mel's waffles. They're so light and fluffy, and since it was a special occasion, Mom even let me put as much whipped cream and chocolate sauce on them as I wanted!

We didn't get to bed until about 2 a.m.—that's the latest I've ever stayed up. The last thing Dad said to me when he was tucking me in was that 2 a.m. used to be an early bedtime for him when he was in college, but he's not in college anymore, so I'd better stay in bed good and long on Christmas morning so he can get his beauty sleep. (Side note: I can't wait to go to college so I can stay up super late every night.)

So we all slept in until 10 a.m. Then we went downstairs and had cereal for breakfast. After that, we spent the rest of the morning playing board games in front of the Christmas tree. (Isaac dominated in Yahtzee just like he always does. I would accuse him of cheating, but how could a five-year-old cheat at dice?) Dad made grilled cheese and tomato soup for lunch, then we all bundled up to play outside where we built the best snow fort in the history of snow architecture—complete with a seven-foot slide made entirely out of snow. After hot chocolate to warm up, we headed over to Mrs. Winkle's for dinner. Guess who else was there, Diary? Yep, none other than "Let Lester make you a deal" himself—Mr. Johnson. I am finally warming up to the idea that Mr. Johnson and Mrs. Winkle are friends. It still weirds me out when they flirt with each other. But if it makes them happy (and if Mrs. Winkle can keep Mr. Johnson from being such a grouch), then I'm okay with it. And if they get married, I'd definitely be first in line to be the flower girl, right? (Side note: I'd better start dropping hints A.S.A.P.)

For dinner, Mrs. Winkle made a fascinating dish she called ham loaf ("I don't like ham, dear, but I like to stay somewhat traditional for Christmas," she said with a grin). For side dishes she served jalapeño cornbread and tortilla chips with mango-chili salsa and guacamole. Other than Mom's dinner rolls that we brought, it was the most nontraditional but oddly delicious Christmas dinner I've ever had or could've imagined.

In the past, I might have decided whether or not I had a "good" Christmas by how many presents I got, but not this year. I received something way better than toys or books or a new pair of Converse All Stars: I got to do something big and important. I helped a family who didn't expect to be helped. We shared with the McCallisters, who now have a little more joy on Christmas and a little more hope for the future. I didn't change the world (yet), but I changed the world for just a moment for them.

Oh yeah, back to the no-presents thing: I didn't think I was going to get any presents, but Mom and Dad had one special surprise for me when we got home a few minutes ago. It's a silver, star-shaped locket that opens on a hinge, and engraved inside it says:

I have big plans for you, EJ.

Trust and follow Me,

and we'll do amazing things together.

Love, God

Let's do it!

EJ

About the Author

Annie Tipton made up her first story at the ripe old age of two when she asked her mom to write it down for her. (Hey, she was just two—she didn't know how to make letters yet!) Since then she has read and written many words as a student, newspaper reporter, author, and editor. Annie loves snow (which is a good thing because she lives in Ohio), wearing scarves, sushi, Scrabble, and spending time with friends and family.

Don't miss book 2,
Church Camp Chaos,
coming March 2014!

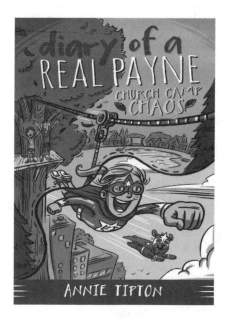

Fun-loving EJ Payne dreams up even more fantastic adventures for herself—promising colossal fun as you become part of her daydreams in *Church Camp Chaos!*

Visit my facebook page to keep up with my latest antics, diary entries, contests, and more! (Make sure it's okay with your parents first!)
WWW.FACEBOOK.COM/DiaryofaRealPayne